The Final Era

Daniel Drake

Opening Credits

My first full-length novel.

I really hope this doesn't suck.

I wrote the first draft of this book about three years ago. I let it sit on my shelf for about two years because I kept telling myself this book isn't that good and it was just cathartic to get some real-life situations onto a page (as well as cram in as many heavy metal references as I could; see how many you can find!).

As people read it and offered me words of encouragement and praise, I got more and more confident about this work; I was confident people would care a little bit about it.

As I wrote it, I realized this was a goddamned trilogy.

Ugh. Now we all have to suffer.

The fun really came when I went back to it after a couple of years. When the first draft wrapped up, it was merely a novella. I thought, "Well, I'm just a short story/novella guy. Whatever. I'll never write the epics! I'll never be famous for having deeply detailed worlds, because that's all books are: tomes!"

Anyways, as I went through the story kept growing and expanding and, sure enough, it's now a novel. I did it, Ma!

I also went through a crisis of confidence when finalizing this work. I felt like my sadder, more tragic takes weren't welcome and that everything had to be happy.

Fuck that.

Get ready for depression.

I was galvanized by reading works from John Steinbeck, by watching shows like Breaking Bad and Better Call Saul from the mighty Vince Gilligan. It made me realize tragedy has a place and that tragedy makes for some of the greatest and most classic works.

And this is a tragedy, so buckle up.

I would like to thank everyone (there's too many to name) who brought me here, whether through helping me learn proper language in school, reading my book in its various states, supporting me in any way with my last work (In Worlds Alone, on Amazon now!), supplying wonderful cover art (I will specifically thank Alec here), or anything else I can't think of, thank you so, so much.

I really hope you enjoy this work.

And don't forget to like, subscribe, and hit that bell-

Wait.

Wrong thing.

Prologue

Falling out of orbit, an asteroid twice as tall as Mount Everest hurtles towards the earth. Ruthless, emotionless, lifeless.

The rocky celestial body enters the planet's atmosphere. This one isn't like the ones that enter almost daily; not the small fragments of about three feet that hit and explode almost every day with no ill effects. Not like the ones where you could find small remnants, small meteorites, as keepsakes, ones where the world would carry on like nothing happened. Not even one the size of an apartment that would only destroy a small city. Not even one the size of a twenty-story building that would flatten a small country.

No, this is an asteroid with the size to extinguish a world and everything that lives.

Not that anything living understands what's happening and, even if they did, they have grown too complacent. Not that the asteroid understands this motive; it's a mercenary without a conscience tasked to do a job, and a job it will do very well.

Dust and smoke rise on the planet below. Sunlight is obscured. The temperature starts to drop. There is no detection, observance, or defining of the rock above. There is no training for such a phenomenon. They cannot change the course of this asteroid.

The asteroid feels no sympathy towards anything living. It is here to finish a job and it creeps ever closer, with flames beginning to surround it, as it approaches landing.

It leaves behind a wicked indent; ninety-three miles in diameter. It leaves no life behind. The planet is wiped clean, a blank slate, scorched earth.

Time to start anew.

Life begins again.

6

Act I: "When the World Screams"

Daniel Drake

December 21st, 2012

"How are you today?"

The stranger David Renninger tried to converse with at Comics Planet kept a concentrated stare down toward his phone and walked by him as if he were an apparition. It was the usual response, so he was not offended. He would not let it affect him, especially not after this month.

At the start of the month, after a couple months of deliberation, interviews, and waiting, waiting, waiting, he was announced by the powers that be as the new General Manager of the Cold Creek Cosmos, a professional baseball team in the PBL.

"This is a new era for the Cosmos!" David exclaimed at his coronating press conference. "I grew up watching baseball greats grace this illustrious team like Rory Silverstein, Jesse Jorgenhammar, Thom Crenshaw, and many, many more. I plan to bring that greatness back to the amazing city that I grew up in and back to the team I've loved since I was a kid. I plan to bring back a winning culture, now and in the future!"

Those prognostications, of course, brought forth the ire of the internet community of fans that rooted for the team, seemingly not believing a word he said, and who could blame them? After years of middling mediocrity, collapses, and failed promises, David couldn't help but expect this. He was a longtime fan before getting this dream job and knew the plight of deep-seated anger they felt. At the end of the day, he knew actions spoke louder than words.

His celebrations as the new General Manager were put on hold very quickly, though, due to the fact that The Winter Summit, an annual event where big trades and free agent signings came to fruition, came to Nashville right after his swearing in. David was thrown headlong into the fire, but he did not flinch. He proved himself immediately by going after Japanese pitching sensation Akio Ito and inking him to a blockbuster deal. He dumped Jordan Hays, a failed signing by the previous regime, onto the Marooners, albeit having to eat most of his gaudy contract to make the deal happen. He dodged Alfred Gonzales' long-term demands of ten years, an absurd commitment to a player already over the hill and past his prime at the age of thirty, while signing veterans Cole Bax and Mark Burns for desperately needed starting rotation depth (especially with how beleaguered their starting five were the year prior). He, also, signed seasoned pros Arik Knoll and John Pier to help on the offensive side which filled gaps offensively and defensively, respectively, left behind by Jordan Hays, and others. His team was rife with young up-and-comers from the farm system while simultaneously infused with veteran knowhow, the latter brought forth by some of his signings. Not to mention, huge game changers like Akio Ito.

David was ready to win the World's Crown and fan support was finally gaining traction; they truly believed he was the savior of this team after many long years of false prophets. They wholeheartedly thought that David would lift the 'curse' placed on this team. Not that David believed in curses, he thought them to be silly, but whatever helps them.

Even though it did help that he was garnering support from fans after his hard work at The Winter Summit, this wasn't the reason he was so elated today.

Tonight, he would propose to his long time girlfriend, Joyce; that was why he was at Comics Planet.

That was part of the reason he wanted to talk with the stranger; he was holding Dark Victor, the graphic novel that Joyce saw him holding the first day they met and then proceeded to extend conversation with him. The other part was him feeling as giddy as a school child and bursting at the seams with excitement and just wanted to talk to anything that breathed.

Thankfully, he could talk to Sam, his longtime friend and the owner of the store, shortly.

Dark Victor was the sequel to The Long Thanksgiving, a story they both read, loved, and bonded over. They continued to talk about how it took David forever to find it and was happy he finally did, which led to them talking about other favorite stories about The Bart and more. She finally told him to enjoy it and walked away. It was love at first sight for David, although he wasn't sure if it was for her, but he should've asked for her number all the same. He was bummed he didn't have the courage, but it was moot after fate threw him a bone later on.

The passerby was a customer of Comics Planet and he figured he could get into a good conversation with another fan like himself, but he guessed that's just how people are.. Upon further thinking, David was now convinced that he just bought the graphic novel for someone else after receiving a text. Oh well, nothing a mere mortal like himself could do to change it; he forgave him and moved on.

Comics Planet had moved into a bigger spot during the whirlwind of The Winter Summit; this was David's first time at the new location. The previous spot was in some crappy mall that felt more like a hole in the wall than an actual store. The ridiculously tiny place the store inhabited the last time he was here was cramped; they had lines of comic boxes on the sides lining the two walls, smothering and depressing white walls at that, and a register on the far side. Upon David stepping into the new location, one thought came to mind: there's elbow room!

On the whole, the brand new location was a much bigger spot. It took the place of an old book store, which admittedly David would miss, but he was happy to see his best friend, Sam, keep succeeding with his business. The walls were painted an almost-as-boring-as-the-previous-white blue and there were more stands for the graphic novels than previously; Sam was finally able to expand his stock and fill his shelves with more GD Comics and independent companies, like Portrait, instead of mostly Wonder Comics. There were more tables set up for old backlogged issues and shelving for the new and previous weeks' comics.

"Davey!" Sam Atkinson shouted. The former comic book artist resided behind the cash register awaiting David's embrace. This was the first time they had seen each other since David's promotion.

Sam got his start doing independent comics with his then-girlfriend, now wife, Liz. They had met on a meet-up app for a group to discuss comics, and became two halves to a whole: Liz was the writer and Sam was the drawer. They created all of the titles they could on the independants (companies such as Portrait and others) like kid-friendly books such as Kick-Butt

Barry to serious as can be titles like Eliminator (that later became its own television series) and Armageddon. After they gained notoriety, they moved on to write and draw for the big two: Wonder and GD. They wrote and drew for Captain Kazakhstan, Captain Wonder, Investigator Comics, Exertion Comics, and plenty more. There were too many to name, that's how successful they were.

That was all behind them these days, though. They opened this store after they told David and Joyce, during one of their ritualistic game nights, that they had basically run out of ideas for books. On top of that, they weren't really happy with the hectic schedule of time constraints and deadlines. "It smothered the creative process after a while." Sam told them, "The big two worked together on ruining our dreams!" he joked. They definitely had plenty of money to fall back on with the TV series royalties they were still receiving and the sales of the books going up with each passing season of the show. But, they still needed something so they decided to start this business. It was something that kept them busy and it still kept the passion of comics alive in some shape for them. It gave them both joy to help comic fans find what they were looking for and to see the look on a customer's face leaving with the perfect book was fulfilling in a new way for them both. It felt like a natural progression for Sam and Liz. Plus, it was a nice supplement for cash.

Sam was a short, stout man that had a full beard down to his collarbones; he had balding, curly brown hair. He's the polar opposite to his buddy David, who was tall and slender with a full head of black hair and clean shaven, despite being relatively the same age.

"Sam!" David shouted back as he went to hug Sam. "Long time, no see. How the hell are ya?"

"Doing well! Hey, I never got to say it in person, but congrats on that promotion! Well earned, my friend!"

"Thank you so much!" David replied with genuine sincerity. "It was a lot, still is, but I love it. It's a dream come true to finally reach my goal as a general manager. And for my favorite team no less! I gotta imagine this is how you felt after your first comic was published."

"I'd have to imagine so. I was honestly shedding elated tears for it. Flipping the pages of your own work is… something I can't describe. No matter how many times I got my work published, it never got old." Sam trailed off for a second, but got back on track. "I hope you get that same feeling every day going to work or signing somebody or whatever the hell you do." Sam laughed. He was not as big of a sports guy as David. "Anyways, you definitely fell behind on your comics while you were gone."

Sam reached for David's bin, number fifty-two, to grab David's ever growing collection of issues that mounted over The Winter Summit. David sorted through them which included: Investigator Comics, Bart and Rob, Verdant Bow, The Beam, Adolescent Dreadnoughts, Alakazam!, Captain Kazakhstan, and Protectors of the Planet. David was more of a GD guy, since it beat Wonder with the first six titles to Wonder's measly latter two.

"Here, you forgot one." Sam said after reaching from under the counter.

David looked at it and it was the story he commissioned from Sam and Liz as a marriage proposal to Joyce (they came out of retirement just for David). It was called "Diamond in the Rough." It was about an explorer looking for a lost diamond, reminiscent of Mausoleum Marauder or Undiscovered, who tracked the long road to a lost and invaluable diamond, which he finally found in a dark cave. A victory in the dark, if you will. Joyce and David bonded over video games, like the ones aforementioned, and more as well as comics and books. As much as he loved sports, he loved the reprieve of nerd culture that Joyce let him indulge in.

"Thank you so much!" he said as he flipped through the beautifully drawn and penned comic book in his hands. "How much do I owe you and Liz?"

"Are you kidding?" Sam brushed it off with a wave. "It's free! Anything for you two!"

"Are you sure? I feel wrong not paying for this hard work."

"Don't feel bad. I'm positive. You owe me nothing for that." Sam subtly changed the subject. "Still having the New Year's party, right?"

"You know I am! Board games and booze are always fun! And the booze is on me." David held up the comic Sam and Liz gifted him. "The only thing stopping this party is the world ending!" he joked as he left the store.

David was at home cleaning the dishes in the kitchen; the kitchen was tiled and held a circular dining table at the center, which was sat in front of a short, fat, and wide mirror. The fridge was to the left and the sink, which David presided at, was in front of cabinets and drawers. David went to polish off the spice rack he had been working on; he was way too proud of that spice rack. Everything looked immaculate, clean, and pristine. He definitely did not like letting work build up or not doing it at all; he loved to keep everything in order.

After he had finished cleaning, he moseyed on over to the mirror in the kitchen and fixed himself up a bit. His normally well-kept, slicked back, black hair was a tad unruly. He noticed a stain on his shirt; it had to have been from the dishes. His piercing, blue eyes stared back at him. David could tell why Joyce fell in love with him, he thought and laughed to himself.

Joyce interrupted his thoughts as she walked in through the front door of their home. Their house was nice and quaint, nothing flashy, but everything they needed. As one entered through the front door there were tall, skinny mirrors on the wall across from it for unknown reasons (they seemed integral to the structural integrity of the house). The L-shaped couch was against said wall and faced the coffee table, as well as the TV on a stand which housed gaming systems, and a bookshelf of games next to it. There was a desk to the side wall with a computer on it for Joyce's clothing business, named The Garb Rack.

The walkway to the kitchen was tile, as was the kitchen that was straight ahead. The space where the couch was was carpeted green. Before the kitchen was a walkway to the left that led to three rooms to the left: a bathroom, a guest room, and the master bedroom.

Joyce was a handful of inches shorter than David, and had long blond hair. She was slender, wore glasses, and today wore jeans, a blouse, and thigh length, woolen lapel coat.

They gave each other a peck on the lips. "Is that what I think it is?" David pointed to the solitary plastic Game Emporium bag around Joyce's forearm.

"It sure is." Joyce smiled; David would never get tired of that smile. "How long have we been wanting to sit down and play Superb Claudio Bros. U?"

"Far too long!" Alongside David's recent uptick in work, Joyce was also enormously busy with her store, due to it being the holiday season, and her working at a mall.

"I'm going to get into my pajamas and play this. Care to join me?"

"You had me at hello." David smiled.

"I never said hello." They both laughed.

They promptly got into their pajamas and onto the couch so quickly that it seemed like they only had tonight to play this game. With their work schedules, that could very well have been the case.

They got done with the first world, but the power went out as they started the second one. Luckily, they didn't get too far in the first level of the second world. Doubly lucky that it autosaved right before they started the new level, so nothing was lost.

"Ah, crud," Joyce said, "the power is out. I wonder if anything severe caused it."

"Probably not." David stated pragmatically as he wrapped her up in his arms.

"What did you think of it so far?" Joyce asked.

"I liked it." David responded. "I just don't know if it'll be able to top the previous version."

"Yes! That one was incredible!" she replied, and then, gesturing vaguely to the kitchen where the Comics Planet bag she saw earlier resided,asked, "What was the haul this week?"

He went out to grab the bag of goodies he got earlier today. David also grabbed her a glass of water, with purpose.

When fate threw him a bone, he was at the bar with Sam and Liz talking about how he would never find the one and how he probably let that one slip through his fingers a week ago, when he spoke with Joyce about Dark Victor and didn't get her number. He was already semi-buzzed at that point, so he needed to sober up to avoid a dreadful morning.

"Water." David asked the barkeep.

"Stiff drink. Don't get too wild." A voice said behind him.

It was Joyce.

"Even on the rocks too." She joked.

David laughed, entranced by her smile. He almost forgot to respond, but he finally did. "I'm a party animal."

She chuckled and said to the barkeep "Put it on my tab." She winked at David.

So after talking for a little while longer at the bar, he took a leap of faith and decided to put his arm around her, making his move. She loved it, a little to his surprise, and the rest was history.

"The haul was far too much. I don't think I can physically read all of those before I go back to work." He said from the kitchen.

"Shh. No work talk." She smiled slyly as David reentered the room.

He handed Joyce the glass of water as he sat down next to her once more. "Figured I'd finally repay the debt." He winked back.

"How thoughtful of you." She jokingly replied, not exactly sure what he meant at the moment, but wanting to play along. A memory started to ping vaguely in her mind and now she remembered what he meant. Joyce wondered why David brought it back around now. Unless…

David pulled out the stack of comics and showed her the haul, "I'm way behind. I did get this new book, though, and it's amazing!"

"What is it?"

"It's called 'Diamond in the Rough.' It's about a treasure hunter."

"So like Undiscovered or Mausoleum Marauder?"

In that moment, David thought to himself how much he loved her. He had no doubt in his mind anymore.

"Exactly! You have to read it!"

"Right now?!"

"Yes! You have to. It's only a one-shot, so the story will be done and over with." Joyce finally submitted and began to read the comic while David departed for the kitchen.

The ring was left in a kitchen drawer, maybe not the safest place, but that's where he left it. He read it a million times while Joyce was at work to get his timing right for when to reenter the room, so he hoped he was right. David read the story so much that he almost began to hate it and then he wondered how much that happened to Liz when she wrote and edited things. His mind was trailing off trying to deal with the worry of the proposal; he had to refocus.

David sauntered back into the living room, hoping he was correct. He was. It was perfect timing. Joyce had just finished reading the comic with tears welling in her eyes as he dropped to a knee.

"Will you marry me?" He asked.

"Yes!" She jumped up from the couch. "A thousand percent yes!"

David put the ring on her finger and rose to meet her kiss. What a great month.

The Final Era

He always marveled at the circular shape of the carrots inside the chicken noodle soup; it was more of a delicacy than the chicken or the noodles.

The bowl was large, almost too large, and it was as long as the cloth underneath to absorb the heat. He still touched the bowl, steadying it against the submerging spoon, even against his Grandma's instructions not to, because he was ready to dig into the best soup on the planet.

Everything from the taste, to the broth with its little bubbles, to the round, wooden table, to the wooden chair, to the small box TV in the corner, to his Grandma's warning, it felt like home…

December 31st, 2012

"…the solar storm we experienced on December 21st was the cause of the widespread blackouts we experienced that day. It is believed to be twice the size of the solar storm of 1859, otherwise known as the Carrington Event…"

David trailed off from the news as he went to the kitchen to check on the dinner he was making for the New Year's Party tonight. He was making BBQ ribs, broccoli, and sweet potatoes for the night ahead while also grabbing himself a Teal Sun beer. Looking out of the window in the kitchen, he saw that the freezing rain was still coming down. He made his way back to the living room, placed his beer on the table, and grabbed the controller preparing to kickstart the WebFilmz app built into his TV to supply background noise while he made some quick work calls, as long as Sam and Liz weren't early, which he didn't bank on, with how crummy the roads probably were due to the freezing rain. But Sam usually always found a way to get there early.

"...upon the solar storm, many of the people that called for doomsday, the end of the world due to the cutoff of the Mayan Calendar, have abruptly taken their own lives." This caught David's attention and he postponed launching the streaming service.

The feed switched to numerous gravesites and then to burning buildings, which were apparently set ablaze by madmen, taking their own lives, while taking more with them to the great beyond. Why are people killing themselves in such vast numbers? David thought. And why are they taking innocent lives with them? What was making people so mad? It just didn't make sense. He couldn't believe what he was seeing.

It seemed acutely selfish to David that people would take their lives after such vile acts, but he didn't want to see this so he pressed the down arrow to change the channel which happened to be another news channel.

Breaking news shifted across the feed. "Reports are coming in of a suicide bombing at a church in Texas." The new reporter on his screen said.

Again, David was baffled. He's never been religious, even though he thought something was out there, but even still he never could see this viewpoint, especially to this extreme. Let people believe what they want to and leave others alone is what he thought.

David finally cleared off his Live TV app and changed it to WebFilmz; he popped on Eliminator, the TV show based on the comic Sam and Liz published together, season eight. He knew this would get a rise out of Sam later on.

Before he could even dial a number, there came a knock on the door. It was Sam and Liz. How shockingly unshocking that they were on time, David thought.

"Hey!" shouted Sam and Liz simultaneously.

David echoed the sentiments, "Man, you still got here early, even with roads as bad as they are. Even for you, this is impressive." He laughed. "Glad you guys made it okay, though." He said earnestly. All three of them embraced each other and David motioned for them to come inside.

"Not on time unless I'm ten minutes early." David loved how strongly Sam felt about punctuality. "But yeah, those roads were quite tetris today."

"Don't you mean treacherous?" Liz asked, even after all these years, Sam could fool her with sarcasm. Or, maybe she was playing along and adding to the bit.

"Like the game? No, the roads are tetris, not treacherous."

"Tetris is the game. It's important to me that you know that." Liz referenced a favorite TV show of all of theirs while backhanding his bicep softly and lovingly. She turned to David. "Where's Joyce?"

"Joyce is just finishing up with... umm… whatever she's doing. I can't quite remember, honestly." David laughed. "We can still get the party started."

Sam snorted, "Looks like you got the party started already." He motioned to the Teal Sun on the coffee table. "Can't believe you drink piss like that."

"Says the guy lugging Starry Austere into my house." They both chuckled at that.

All three of them got situated on the couch as Joyce came in and took part in the same friendly greetings David, Sam, and Liz just partook in, except for one special thing.

"Guess what?" Joyce brandished her left, ring finger which was now bedazzled with jewelry. "Even though you probably already knew. Can't imagine where else David would have gotten that comic from."

"That's amazing!" Liz exclaimed with delight. "I knew about it, but I didn't know the ring would be so nice." She turned to Sam with a smirk. "Why didn't you get me a nice one?"

"I'm just a comic shop owner."

"With comic book royalties." Liz dramatically rolled her eyes.

"Which clearly isn't much, with how shitty the show is becoming." He pointed to the TV playing Eliminator, which got some smiles.

"Want me to grab you something to drink? We got water, juice, or milk." Joyce asked.

"The milk is homemade." David delivered in deadpan and sealed with a wink to Sam.

After a brief period of belly laughter, Sam responded. "I'll be alright for now."

"What are we thinking tonight?" Liz asked as Joyce joined them on the couch.

"We just got the new Claudio Bros. game. We could all jump on each other wildly and die for a bit." joked Joyce, which got a satisfying reaction from them all. They did end up playing it, which led to exactly what Joyce predicted: them jumping off of each other and sacrificing each other to the bottomless pits on the levels and running out of time in the allotted time limits of each level. It was good fun.

After that, while Liz went out to smoke, with Joyce joining her to chat, Sam pulled out his phone and showed David his latest project. It was an arcade machine he had been building from scratch. Sam showed him the buttons he had already purchased along with the various drillings he had done to get the perfect sized holes for said buttons and joysticks in the console. Sam was always making something.

"So how will you get the games for it?" David asked.

"Well, it's something called a NostalgicQuiche, and it's really neat. It has all the games on it and I just hook it up to the unit and it'll play the games. I'll of course need to get a TV to lay flat to broadcast the games so it can actually be played, but one step at a time." Sam stated matter-of-factly.

The two ladies made their way back in from the windy, rain soaked night and made their way to the game room downstairs in the basement, without a word to David or Sam.

The basement was a small, carpeted room that had two long shelves, with bins containing various board games.

"So this isn't…" Liz made a motion as if she was reloading a shotgun and pointed to the ring, "…right?"

"Oh, god no." Joyce laughed.

"You know I kid. Kind of." Liz said. "Are you ever going to try for them?"

Joyce always loved this about Liz. She was nosey, but no one ever really asked her about these things, so she was happy to indulge. "Maybe someday.

We've been so preoccupied with building our careers that it hasn't really happened yet. How about you?"

"No way." Liz definitively stated. "You think I want to ruin our great life with little mongrels?" They both laughed. Joyce could see some logic in their thinking, but she was still undecided.

Joyce brought her focus back to the games on the shelves. "How about this?"

"Great choice." They raced back up the steps.

"Are you gonna mount it on the wall or get support legs underneath it?" David asked Sam upstairs.

"I was thinking of mounting it, but our walls are garbage so I think I will end up doing the latter."

Sam's presentation was put on pause as Liz and Joyce came hustling up the stairs.

"Sorry to interrupt the geek meeting, but," Liz smiled as she held up the game Catchlines, "you wanna play?"

"You wrote comics and you call us nerds?" David smiled as he turned to Sam; Sam agreed it was a good point, even though he was the artist of said comics, so he said nothing.

"Yeah, and you buy 'em and I make money, nerd." Liz laughed again. "So, do you wanna play?"

"Of course we do."

So they made their way to the kitchen and played some Catchlines. It went how it usually did: they got a few more beers deep, so David deliberated on answers he already knew to screw the other team by draining the clock, and then it petered out and shifted into talking between the four.

"You always do that when we play! So unfair, man!" Sam said.

"Gotta play chess, not checkers." David responded.

"But we played Catchlines!"

That elicited more eye rolls than laughter, and most of the latter was from Sam. Dinner was ready after they had gotten done with that round and David virtually inhaled his meal.

"You really put a hurtin' on that." Sam said as he finished his meal, minutes after David.

"Yeah, I'm a growing boy." David joked.

After everyone else was done, David gathered up all of the plates and deposited them in the sink.

"I could've taken care of that, since you made dinner and all." Joyce said.

David kissed the top of her head. "It's not a problem." He smiled as he grabbed her plate.

"Here, before I forget," Sam said as David sat back down, "a late Christmas present."

"Oh, you didn't have to do this! You already helped with the greatest moment of our lives." David replied.

"Well, I didn't. It's from Santa." Sam quipped.

He opened the gift wrapping, seemingly worthless. David didn't understand why people didn't just use a bag, but it seemed like a weird hill to die on when someone is giving you something.

He opened the package and found an expansion to one of his favorite board games: Lilliputian; it was an Adult Kung-Fu Tortoise Oddities expansion. He really did love this game (and the Tortoises) mainly for the player interaction, even though the end could drag out with everyone trying to screw each other over, waiting for the final step to unleash havoc.

"Thank you so much!" David said. "We definitely have to play this when we're sobered up."

"So not anytime soon." Sam joked.

"Here I got this for you as well." David handed him the game box (no wrapping) and it was a game called Windfall. It was one neither of them have ever tried, but it held great reviews online. Plus, it involved legumes, so it had to be somewhat enjoyable.

After expressing their gratitude, they opened up David's gift to Sam, saw the rule book was only a page or so describing the ultimate goal of harvesting the most legumes for coins, and decided it was worth a shot. They had a ton of fun learning and playing the game, slightly modifying the rules so they could finish up quicker than normal, since they were already so drunk. Another fun game to add to their collection.

"That was really fun! Can't thank you enough for this!" Sam exclaimed.

"Not a problem at all! Glad you liked it. It truly was fun. How can something so simple be so fun?"

"It's always the simplest things!"

Liz received a buzz on her cell phone. "I should take this."

"Who is it?" Sam asked.

"I think it's from the store."

"At this time of the night?"

Liz shrugged and departed outside.

After what felt like an eternal silence, David tried to change the subject and tried to placate Sam's worries. "I had a really vivid dream last night."

"Oh yeah? What was it?" Joyce asked.

"I was at my grandma's house, as a child, eating her chicken noodle soup. I haven't thought about that in years." He faded away for a second. "I haven't dreamed about her in years. Dreams about her happened mostly around the time she died."

"Well, dreams are pretty random, right." Sam said, more of a statement than a question.

"They can play off of what happened throughout your day sometimes." Joyce said.

"But that was the day I proposed to you, so it doesn't really add up. It was just… odd." David picked up his train of thought again. "It's a really good memory, though. Maybe things have been so good that it reminded me of the only place that felt like home as a child, now that I'm finally, fully at home now. I have my dream job and now I'm engaged." David smiled at Joyce. She returned an even warmer smile.

"Maybe the solar storm affected you." Sam joked. "Were you able to witness it last week?"

"It was beautiful." Joyce responded, gazing mournfully at the dreary night, "It was like the light covered the entire sky. Unspeakable beauty"

"The unspeakable beauty had the complete opposite effect on the world, though." David added, "Did you see these nutjobs killing themselves? Taking others with them? Maybe the Mayans were right."

"I was just joking, but yeah, all of that stuff has been truly terrible and unspeakable." Sam responded, agreeing with the horror of the world currently.

"Indeed," Joyce agreed as well, "but as awful as I might sound I feel there should be some sort of empathy shown to them."

David was perplexed. "How? What do you mean?"

"People deal with life differently. With pain differently. Maybe this was bubbling for sometime underneath it all. I'm in no way advocating or romanticizing suicide and definitely not taking others with them, but still, there's more untold." Joyce liked to see the good in all, through any amount of blackness. She was a caregiver at heart. "Being empathetic and forgiving is something the world needs more of. Maybe now more than ever."

"I can kind of see where she's coming from." Sam said, aligning himself with her or just merely straddling the fence. "Plus, it's not like anything is a natural death. In my opinion, at least, old people will die simply from neglect and indifference rather than suicide or drugs."

"Even if there's no natural death," David interjected, "it still doesn't make this right."

"We're not saying it does." Joyce responded.

"I was just making a general point on the subject at hand." Sam shrugged.

"Everyone deals with things in different ways," Joyce picked back up her thought thread as if it never stopped, "if not all healthy. People end it all because they can't take it or slowly end it through drugs. Or maybe their entities couldn't take anymore."

"Their entities?" David asked.

"Yeah, basically one entity is living every potential point of consciousness. It's infinite reincarnation and the entity jumps from point to point, body to body, when one form 'deactivates' or 'dies' and another 'activates' or 'is born' until it's reached the end of all things possible."

"I'm still a bit confused." David said.

"So basically semi-immortal and virtually no death. But maybe some of them are reaching their ultimate end and it is finally catching up to some of them.”

“You actually believe that?” David, ever defiant. Or just bored. But mostly drunk.

“Never said I did. It’s just a thought I got from somewhere a while back. Something interesting to think about. No one really knows what’s at play.”

“Either way, it’s still infectious.” David retorted with his truth and pragmatic point of view. “There’s nothing to gain and everything to lose. It has a ripple effect on everyone involved. People who love you suffer eternally because of your death, whether you bring it about through suicide or drug use or whatever. We live in such a degenerate culture that it will be the end of us. No one cares about the consequences, only what appeases their selfish needs.”

“How can you say something so rash and generalize everyone?” Joyce asked, honestly not understanding how he could view things as so black and white. “You have not and will never know these people, their darkness, them at their most vulnerable. You pass people every day you know nothing about.”

“Sonder.” Sam punctuated her point.

“It’s all black because they make it that way. To appease themselves and no one at all.” David said.

“There’s more gray than you think.” She responded to his claim.

“I don’t see it at all.”

"See, that's kind of your issue David." Sam retorted, laced with some venom to appease his anger for now. He knew David can get argumentative, especially with some alcohol, but it still got him going. "You don't actually wanna hear any different side, you wanna hear what you prescribe and that's it. You tend to belittle every other opinion but yourself."

"But I believe it's wrong, and isn't that my right?" David claimed, keeping his cool. He was used to poking the bear on these topics. He enjoyed challenging people and seeing their sides of the coin.

"It is, but I believe thinking it's wrong in your own solitude is fine, but outright shutting it down from another person's perspective isn't right. Everyone is shaped by their own life." Sam claimed, and continued by adding, "I'm an atheist, through and through, and while I don't believe what she says, I would gladly talk to her about it, but you'd rather shout over her."

David steamrolled over the accusations and continued, "Since you're an atheist, how do you find purpose at all? If there's no point, being an atheist, why live?" He loved asking these questions, what made people tick.

"To enjoy what we have. To live my life to the fullest. I don't view myself as special, in a grander scheme, but I believe we matter to each other. To you two and to my wife." Sam pointed to the two at the table and in the general direction of Liz outside.

"So you still believe in something?"

"Not a deity, and that's basically all religion comes down to. I believe in my own universe, and that matters to me and me alone, and some select others that I care about, of course. There's a belief in life and a belief in god. Two different things. Christians pray all the time, not believing in 'his' plan and questioning 'him,' so by your logic of me believing in something negating atheism, every Christian is a little Atheist, since they pray and defy 'his' plan." Sam defended his belief. Then he questioned David. "So, I'll ask now, what do you live for?"

"I can't say I've found that yet." David responded, ever doubting anything and everything around him.

For all of David's fire and for him to say something so simple made Sam stifle a laugh, but he held his composure. "Fair enough. I think we're all a little agnostic, but I don't think it negates anything about us." Sam paused, but quickly continued, "Sorry if I got upset, but you've put down my atheistic ways numerous times before and that's why I don't bother with talking to you about it anymore." Sam was genuinely apologetic. He knew David was wrong, but even still, he did not like to be upset or have anyone upset.

"Don't worry about it; I should be apologizing to you since you're right. So, I'm sorry." David pleaded his innocence and went on, "You know how I can get sometimes. I just like asking these things and I genuinely don't mean to upset anybody. One last thing," David smiled, "I just don't understand how you can believe that there's nothing. That it's all happenstance." David pondered, not wanting the conversation to end prematurely. Then again, he could talk all night about stuff like this.

"Alright, but this is it. Like I said before, I don't view myself as special. I'm just living like any other animal until I die. That's our primal directive: live and survive. There's nothing more irritating to me than someone viewing their life as something important when there's such cacophony throughout the world. Like what we were just talking about with these mass killings and suicides."

David conceded, with a nod, and said, "Listen, I know I sound like a dick or an asshole about this, but when I seemingly belittle everything, it's because I like to challenge everybody, see how they think, as well as challenge everything and doubt it all. Plus, it's all kind of a big joke, right? Philosophy, religion, all of it. I like to think about it but does it really matter? At all? Thinking about the after is kind of pointless. I do and I don't care about it, if that makes any sense."

Sam couldn't stifle the laugh this time. "You made us all get worked up and then say that?" He paused briefly. "I do get it, though."

"As do I." Joyce joined in.

"Let's drink some more." David smiled. They said cheers, clinking their glasses, and ended the conversation with a hearty drink.

Sam loved to think about stuff like this, but it was exhausting actually talking about it with others, as weird as that sounded. You couldn't change people's minds, so what's the point? Sam knew David loved these talks, though, so he indulged him.

They were all a bit exasperated, but at least they terminated it on a good note. They all decided at once, without speaking, that they needed some fresh air and got up to meet Liz outside.

It was still incredibly chilly outside; the winds of winter howled and blasted their exposed faces, as the grass crunched under their feet. The bitter night's conditions enveloped David and everyone else.

"What was the call about?" Sam asked Liz as he joined her and sat on the rock outside in the patio area. There were two lawn chairs opposite, which sat near the house's walls, which David and Joyce occupied.

"One of our employees. Tristan." Liz laughed, which surprised Sam (he thought it would be a more serious call). "He accidentally set off our new security system. Most of the call was just him apologizing profusely to me."

"Well, at least you know the money you spent on it was worth it." Joyce smiled.

"Yeah, we're catching our own guys." Sam joked as Liz fell into his chest. "And here I thought it was a real break-in." He turned to David. "I was about to say you were right about it being infectious."

David nodded but fell silent; he guessed that the drinks were catching up to him. He was jealous of Sam at this moment, nestled up with his love. David hoped he hadn't upset Joyce too much. She felt far away from him tonight. That, or it was the drinks playing tricks on him.

The night was growing old as it was almost reaching midnight, so Liz and Sam decided to depart. David guessed they wanted to share some personal time as the new year rang in. David was hoping he would get some personal time of his own.

"Are you sure you should drive? With the conditions and the drinks?" David asked.

"Yeah, we'll be fine." Sam motioned in no particular direction. "I'm all sobered up."

"Well, be careful." Joyce said lovingly. "Thanks for the help with the proposal and thanks for coming over again! Text us when you get home."

"We will. Thanks for having us over!" responded Liz. "It's always fun coming over."

"Just make sure you don't forget to bring your beans over next time." David joked, referencing Windfall, the game he had bought Sam.

"I never forget my beans." Sam winked as he bantered back; he was always there to receive a good joke.

———————————

"I didn't make you mad at dinner tonight, did I?" David asked with two minutes to midnight.

"No." Joyce assured him. "You act like I can't take it, because I'm so sweet, but I can. I enjoy it, too. I couldn't have made it this far with you if I didn't."

David smirked. "I love you."

"I love you, too."

"...10, 9..."

"No matter how many times the new year comes, it never gets old bringing it in with you." David was being sappy; maybe because of the drinks or maybe in earnest.

"...6, 5…"

"Now you're trying too hard." Joyce smiled.

'...2, 1...:"

David and Joyce shared a kiss as the new year dawned.

He was on a knee. He was proposing. Although, it was not his girlfriend. Or was it? He knew he was dreaming, but could not do anything to change the path set out in front of him.

He recognized the woman before him, even though it wasn't her. Why? Who was this woman? The room was different; it was smaller, more compact. The house was definitely smaller as well. Was it an apartment? He hadn't lived in one of those for years. Or so he thought.

Nothing he did changed it, the dream played out outside of him and for him, like a theater act. It was a show played by him, for him.

Sudden shift, jarring. The winter is worsening. He's walking through the callous snow, the unrelenting winds. He was alone. Nothing there. Why was he here? He was set out on this path. By himself. For himself. No one else. Why? He doesn't know.

He can't change it. It's the path set out for him, by him. He marches through the snow, step by step...

February 19th, 2013

Today was a special day for David for a couple of reasons: For one, today was the day that pitchers and catchers reported to Springtime Practice which signaled the dawning of the baseball season. Secondly, it was his best friend Sam's birthday. Unfortunately, he would not be able to be there in person; David had to be with the team for the advent of the baseball season. He was able to shoot him a text, at least. One of the few glories of technology.

"Happy birthday, man! Love you, dude! Have a drink for me!" the text read.

David began his day by doing his meditation; he started with this so he could have a cool, calm, and relaxed start to the day and to clear his mind. All in all, he wanted to make sure the control center of his entire body was in complete order, and meditation helped that. After that, he did his afternoon run to keep his body moving and in as good of shape as possible. The human body was meant to move and meant to be active, much like horses for the buggies, so he made sure he did so. It was almost a criminal offense to him if you didn't work out, mentally and physically; a complete disservice to the mind and body.

The weather was bitter on his run. It had been bitter cold for months now, which isn't out of the ordinary for winter, but it was weirder to David since he was down in Florida. He was in San Castle, to be exact; this was where pitchers and catchers reported for Springtime Practice. We were still in winter, David kept telling himself, the last vestiges of it, though, but it should be warmer. Something felt different.

"Thank you, buddy! Love you too!" Sam, a notoriously late texter, got back to him after the run. Sam also sent a picture of his finished arcade machine milliseconds after the text of thanks. David loved it; the machine had a punk-like design to it, including shooting separated eyeballs across the top and various tentacle looking things on the sides. The paint job was a fluorescent green and orange. David wondered if Sam painted this himself. It looked to David that he bought a rolling cabinet to place it on, which he later confirmed in another text. He always marveled at Sam's ingenuity and artistic prowess. No wonder he drew comic books for a living.

"I'm definitely playing that the next time I'm over!" David shot the text back; he was, admittedly, pretty giddy about it.

David arrived at the baseball field where tons of hopefuls gathered for a shot to be on the twenty-five man roster. He donned the Cosmos teal blue and black (but mostly black) polo and brown khaki pants. The pop of the catcher's mitt from a high nineties fastball was blissfully filling his ears. It was a symphony of elation. One of the greatest sounds you could hear, in David's opinion.

He was currently watching his Japanese sensation throw the ball. Akio looked even better up close and personal. He was transfixed by that, but forcefully pulled his gaze to his other signing Cole Bax; he was ageless (currently at the age of forty, but it didn't show), consistent, durable, and reliable while much, much slower in speed than the normal arm in the majors, somewhere in the late eighties for velocity (a Reagan era fastball). His finesse and location were not completely opposite to Akio, as all pitchers should have that, but Akio had far more power than Bax. Roger Alden was different as well; he was an unorthodox knuckleball pitcher, who recently revamped his career and won the Ty Oldesmith Award, which is given to the best pitcher in each league every year. A lot of fans wanted him to accept a trade for him this past offseason, as a way to get two high-level prospects, but David decided against it. He knew better than the armchair managers, anyways, David thought. Alden was a rare talent in his eyes, with his funky pitch. Thom Hardy, the young upstart, turned in an encouraging rookie campaign, and looked to be great for years to come. Mark Burns, Dalton Jee, Johnny Neephew, and Jacoby Hapnor filled out the backend of the rotation; the final four would battle for the last spot in the five-man rotation, with Burns being the front runner. Three would, unfortunately, get the short end of the stick, being long-man relievers in the bullpen, pitchers who go multiple innings in relief for the starter, and spot start for the Cosmos, as needed with injuries, or sent down to the minors. David viewed all three of them as viable men for any rotation, but competition breeds excellence. These weren't the only pitchers in front of him this afternoon, but they were the notables. There were tons of starters and relievers; some hopeful and some guaranteed a spot. Overall, he liked what he saw.

David's thoughts were interrupted as the trainer of the Cosmos began to make his way up to him. "Something looks off with Akio. Do you see it?"

He took in Ito throwing the ball once again. His fastball was definitely not popping as much as it did to start the day. Seemed like something might have been wrong with his elbow.

They both made their way to talk with him. David asked the translator to come with him as well, so he could properly speak to Akio. "Everything all right?" David asked the translator. The translator fed Akio the same question in Japanese.

Ito nodded. He wasn't entirely familiar with the language, but a nod was worldwide.

"We should probably shut him down for now, until we can get an MRI on it. Make sure there is no structural damage." The trainer said to David.

David nodded at that, but disagreed. "He knows his body well, though. Better than any of us. We'll just keep an eye on it." He conceded partially. "Let's just shut him down for the day and we'll get a better look tomorrow." The trainer agreed to that. David turned to the translator to tell Akio Ito the news; he looked somewhat dejected after being told to shut down on the first day of camp. David could understand.

David turned and walked away after that, losing himself in the sound and his thoughts. He was worried about his big signing; he wondered if there might have been damage that was brought over from his years in the Japanese league and it was finally catching up with him. He tried not to worry, so he kept telling himself that it was just an anomaly and Akio would be fine by tomorrow.

This worry was quickly overtaken by seeing the baseballs hit the mitts once more which brought him back to the hopefulness of the year ahead. He was ready to prove the doubters wrong and start the real work on his dream. It was only a matter of time until his team won the World's Crown, in his mind. It was still Sam's birthday, but David felt he was receiving more gifts than him today.

―――――――――

After sending his last text to David, Sam played numerous games on his new toy. The NostalgicQuiche was gifted to him by Liz for his birthday; she knew him too well. It was the final touch on his machine. Sam was frozen in time seeing the sheer amount of games on this little device, almost to the point of not starting anything. Sam laughed at that; of course he was going to play a couple (hundred) of these games.

After testing out the machine across a handful of games (sadly, not a hundred), Sam and Liz had an incredible home cooked meal. The meal consisted of pork chops, green beans, and scalloped potatoes. She was a wiz when it came to cooking and it definitely helped Sam not eat Starving Mans and other such frozen meals nightly. He thanked her immensely tonight, and every night, for that matter, that Liz made meals for him; he did not take any of this for granted. Sam really did love her for all the little things she did for him, including stuff like this.

"How's the new toy?" Liz asked.

"Oh, I love it." Sam said. "There's so much on it, I don't know if I'll be able to play it all!"

"I'm sure if anyone can, it's you." Liz joked back. Sam smiled at that.

"Wouldn't have been possible to finish without you." Sam said lovingly.

"Stop," Liz blushed and rolled her eyes. "It's nothing. You could've bought it yourself." She was never sure how to take a compliment, so she didn't, like she normally does.

"You still did and I love you for it."

She made a kissing motion with her lips as she rose to grab the plates.

"The meal was amazing, too. Like always. How did I get so lucky?" Sam expressed his gratitude whilst rubbing his belly. Liz bent down and kissed his cheek.

"Oh, hush," Liz responded with another eye roll to his insatiable complimenting. "You say that every time."

"Because it's true!" Sam wanted to make sure she was always happy and was never unsure of his love for her. Sam wanted her to know how much everything meant to him; she rolled her eyes for a third time. Liz came back to the side of the table and Sam grabbed her hand. "I really mean it." Liz blushed and Sam rose to kiss her on the lips. Liz's heart was always full around Sam, even if she had a tough time expressing it.

A buzz from Liz's phone on the table ended the tender moment.

"What was that?" Sam asked.

"It's the security system for our store."

"Did we get another of our workers?" Sam smiled.

"It's too late for that." Liz said soberly, even though she fully understood the joke. "I better go check it out." Liz was confident nothing was happening, since the first one was a false alarm, but the worry was still there.

"I can come with you." Sam was also concerned, mainly with the idea of her going alone. He worried for the worst, like always.

"No, it's fine, it's probably just another false alarm. You have a birthday to continue celebrating and a game system that needs playing." It was nearing midnight, so his birthday was about to wrap up, and Liz wanted him to enjoy every second of it and not have to worry about the store. She could bear that cross for the night. It was nothing, anyways.

She rose and planted a kiss on the still seated Sam, grabbed her coat, and departed for the store. Sam escorted her to the door. As the door shut behind her, Sam made his way back to the game room, unsteadily, to play with his newest toy some more.

February 20th, 2013

When Liz arrived at the store, she took a momentary glance at her watch; it was past midnight now, meaning Sam's birthday was officially over and that the store had been closed for hours; no one else would be here, other than whatever tripped the alarm. She kept telling herself it was a 'whatever' and not a 'whoever.' It was nothing.

Her fears were quickly realized as Liz saw a figure through the glass doors, walking around sullenly and creepily. It was picking up various figures, busts, and books and throwing them over their shoulder without a care. Liz rummaged through her purse and realized she had left her phone in the car; she wanted to turn and run, but was locked in place at the thought of the person hearing her scarper and doing something rash. She would have to go inside the store and hit the alarm underneath the counter to alert the police. She rummaged some more and found her knife; she pulled it out and concealed it behind her back, just in case the robber spotted her and made an attempt to attack her. She hoped the robber wouldn't see her out in the hallway of the mall with the light shining from the ceiling above.

Liz hastily pulled out her keys, unlocked the door, and slowly pushed the door open. Luckily, she was silent enough to not be noticed. Or was the figure in such a trance that nothing would have broken their focus? She was upset that they didn't splurge on the security system that immediately notified the police. It would save her from having to try and play hero right now.

As Liz stealthily walked through the tables of comic bins, she heard the figure say, "One last time…" The shadowed figure said it over and over again in a ritualistic fashion.

She crept around to try and gain a view of the stranger. A man, presumably, of average height, wearing a hoodie, with the hood pulled up over his head. She made her way behind the counter to sound the alarm.

While in motion, Liz dropped her knife.

"Who's there?" the figure shouted, in an unsteady voice.

The stranger summoned a gun from his jacket pocket and pointed it in an aimless direction. He stalked and kept saying the same things: "Who's there?" "One last time…" He seemed like he was drifting in and out of consciousness.

Liz hit the alarm after a few ragged breaths and made her way to the back office, with the man going to the front of the store, where the counter was. She was now frightened, but trying not to panic. There was no door leading to the outside from the office, so she would have to wait for the cops or sneak her way out through the high window.

She decided on the latter.

Liz snuck around the counter after she was out of the man's field of vision. She made her way towards the door of the back office, keeping low, and pulled out her keys again, unlocked this door, and slowly plunged the handle down and entered the office.

She picked up the chair at the office desk and moved it towards the wall the window was at. The lack of light in the office would have made it hard to find the window for a random person, but luckily she knew this store by heart and felt it out. She tried the window, but heard the sound of footsteps approaching behind her; the man must have found out quickly that she was no longer behind the counter or he just wandered back here randomly while stuck in his trance. She guessed she was waiting for the police now. Liz gracefully dropped to the ground and hid underneath the desk where one's legs would be if they were sitting normally. She was surrounded by the metal cabinets that were a part of the desk, giving her a brief sense of shelter in the darkness. She began to panic even further when she realized she left her knife where she dropped it; she cursed herself.

Liz tried to steady her breathing as the stranger dragged himself past the side of the desk, gun screeching ominously on the metal above. He slowly made his way around to the side Liz was on; she held her breath. At first, he didn't notice her and Liz hoped she had just won the most terrifying game of hide and seek by sheer luck, but she wasn't so lucky. Even through the blackness, she could see the stranger's deranged eyes descending on her. The man's face was revealed in her mind's eye: eyes bulging out of his head, a smile of a clown, and teeth jagged was what she imagined before her in the night-soaked office.

"Who are you?" the figure asked. Liz imagined the smile evaporating before he said that.

"I'm the owner." she responded, "Who are you? Why are you here?"

The stranger left the consciousness of this earth for some other far from here. "One last time…" the figure said ominously. "One last time…"

"One last time for what?" Liz was petrified.

The figure snapped back to this reality and fixed his gaze back onto her. "I want to feel. One last time… until I end this." The man lowered his gun and put it back into his coat pocket.

"End what?"

"This. Me. All of it." After uttering these words, he pulled out a book of matches as he made his way around to the side of the table again, out of Liz's sight once more. Liz peeked out from underneath the desk and saw the stranger struck one of his matches, lit the box that held the rest of them, and threw it onto a box in the office.

Liz tried to run, but the man was quicker. She peeled through the door and tried to reach the light of the mall corridor just outside of the store, but the stranger made his way to the entryway of the door of the office, silhouetting himself. He loosed off a bullet and it went through her back and out of her heart, draining it of its fullness. She crawled, in the death throes, there was no fight left to give.

The police's sirens wailed outside the store, finally responding to the call, and lights drenched the stranger in red, rhythmic patterns. The flames licked his collar as he stared to face the incoming officers.

"One last time…" Another shot went through his head.

Muddy boots hitting the ground around him. Bullets rained down in sheets. Powder littered the air and overcame his senses. War.

He was in the trenches. His buddy flanks him to his right and he leaves as quickly as he notices him.

His friend doesn't last long. Immediately, his absolution is under fire and taken from him. He would never smell defeat, because no more life would be given to him.

The battleground was his only home, his only meaning in this life. Nothing for him but to survive. Nothing to protect him from the assault before him. Nothing in the foxhole to have his back. He was alone…

A vibration from his phone on the wooden side table startled David awake from another dream in his hotel room. He looked at his phone with one hazy eye and saw that Sam was calling. David saw it was 3:30 in the morning. Why the hell is he calling me so early? David thought.

"Hey, man, what are you doing up at this ungodly hour?" David asked, half-jokingly and groggily.

Radio silence on the other end. Panic and fear rises through Sam's lack of words and the nothingness he offered on the other end.

"Sam? You there?" Still nothing from Sam and the concern rises even more somehow for David; he was now fully awake and alert.

Muffled and silent cries began to emerge on the other end as the century-like seconds passed. Sam could not stifle it any longer. "She's gone." The words almost fell out of his mouth.

David did not want to say it. He did not want to realize the worst possible outcome, but Sam was lost in his cries of despair. Finally, David asked, "What do you mean? Who's gone?"

Sam pushed through his crying, and stated, "...Liz."

"She left you?" Somehow, that reality was better than the one David feared.

"No…"

It was even worse than David imagined. "No, no… it can't be…" David was rendered speechless for a beat. "She's-"

"Gone… I can't believe it…"

David was in utter shock and disbelief. Was he even in the waking state? He wanted to believe this was another dream, like the ones he had been having. Nightmare would be the better word for it, but at least it wouldn't be real.

"What happened?" David asked and knew it was something Sam couldn't work up the gumption to say, so David continued, "I'll be taking the first flight possible to be there with you. I love you buddy, stay strong."

Sam's crying became worse and the call eventually dropped out. David looked at the phone and saw he hung up; it was all clearly too much for him.

The end of the call chilled David. David took no offense to him hanging up; he could not even begin to imagine the loss Sam was going through right now. To lose his significant other, his counterpart, his everything, he could not put himself there. David would not know what to do without Joyce. He immediately felt bad for making this situation about himself and Joyce as opposed to Sam and Liz.

David immediately started to search for flights, but quickly fell into deep sleep. He was not able to stay awake any longer despite the shocking news.

Inside of a cage. No, a cell. Same difference. His head is bowed to the ground and a man enters the room.

"Are you ready?" The man asks. He didn't want to answer. He didn't want to make this a reality.

The man opened the cell door and walked towards him. The man crouched next to him and pushed the button behind his left ear.

The sleeper awakes...

February 24th, 2013

David was granted time away from the team for Liz's funeral and all of the proceedings. They were more caring than ever, which made David happy. At least he found some more family through these bad times. He just wished he could have found this out in a different way, though.

It was difficult, it was trying, all David could do was cry through his brother's eyes for now. He was in shock as well and couldn't process everything he was feeling.

David wanted to show how he felt, but he felt very selfish to do so. It was Sam's time to grieve and not his; Sam didn't need his burden right now. Sam was the foremost priority. David would have to compartmentalize this whirl of pain.

The funeral was to be held today and David didn't know what to expect; he had never known true loss before. He had never been to a funeral before, either, as shocking as it might seem.

Him, Joyce, and Sam had to lean on each other for strength during the uncertain times. David tried his best to talk with Sam, but it was to no avail. He was shutting off and shutting down before his eyes.

It was a closed casket funeral, for obvious reasons. Because of that, Sam would never see her again; that broke David's heart.

David took stock of the fact that they were in a church and part of him wondered what Sam thought of that, if it even crossed his mind. They were seated next to each other, down in front, with the rest of Liz's family.

"I'll miss the pointless conversations, the goofy pictures we'd send each other." Joyce reflected, trying to hold back her pain through her eulogy. She was one of many, including Liz's mother, father, siblings, and friends, who came up to the podium in the church to share their times with the late Liz. It all felt like a blur to Sam; he couldn't remember any of the words that were said.

While Sam barely registered anything, David really marveled at the strength of her parents. Was it strength to hold it in? David didn't know, but that's what he was taught from his elders.

"I'll miss her smile and her personality; they were both one of a kind. I had a dream of her smiling the other day…" Joyce trailed off, but regained her composure. "Through David and then through Sam," she motioned to Sam; his eyes were still glued to the floor below him, "I was able to find my best friend. When we met, it felt like we picked up where we left off in some previous life. I will miss her dearly."

Sam also wrote a eulogy. He was gripping it in his hands next to David, but it was, ultimately, never spoken. David wanted him to stand up and show the world his scars, his pain, leave it out there for all to see, but Sam didn't want to. No matter how much he wanted him to, no matter how unhealthy it was to bottle up (even though David, ironically, did the same), Sam was a stone.

"Are you alright? Please show yourself to me. This isn't healthy." David remembered saying earlier in the day to Sam.

Sam turned to him, welling with tears and filled with agony, and said, "I don't know what you want me to say." He was still in a state of utter shock.

David supposed he couldn't force Sam to do anything he didn't want to.

The funeral passed and family members and friends expressed their sorrows, but it was mostly commandeered by a priest who babbled on about nothing. Anger started to boil inside of David during the priest's, as David thought, bullshit sermon and abhorrent attempts at humor. The funeral came and passed, and it was time to keep moving. For Sam especially, David hoped.

David didn't intend this to be callous; he just didn't think it was healthy to dwell on these types of things. He wanted Sam to be healthy again. He wanted Sam to see hope again. He didn't want Sam to suffer any longer. But he knew he had to grieve as well. It was a process.

"Hey, Sam, did you want to grab something to eat?" David asked outside of the church; it was another brutally cold day. "A drink? Play a game or two?"

Sam was silent.

"Anything." David persisted.

"On us. Please." Joyce agreed.

"I'm good. I gotta go… somewhere." Sam looked up, barely meeting their gaze, and gave a forced smile. He walked towards his car.

"Go… somewhere?" David eyed Joyce after they were left alone.

"That was, indeed, odd." Joyce replied. "But don't think too far into it. He's going through it."

"I know. I just… worry."

"I know you do." Joyce smiled and hugged David a little tighter.

"Keep an eye on him while I'm gone." David said as he turned to Joyce. "Please."

"Of course."

"Keep an eye on yourself, too." He kissed her forehead. It wasn't lost on him how much she cared for him even during her own tumultuous time. "I'm always here if you need anything." Joyce smiled at him and rested her head on his chest. "Am I doing the wrong thing for leaving?" David was basically thinking out loud.

"No." Joyce assured him. "You have to do your job as well. Unfortunately, nothing stops that train."

"You're right."

"Plus," Joyce continued, "it'll be a good distraction. I know you're keeping it tucked deep inside, but you're feeling it, too.

"Also," she continued on, "it's your dream job and you're just starting it. You've worked so hard for this. Don't worry so much about us. It'll take time, but everything will work out."

David wasn't sure if he felt the same. As much as he hoped, Sam did seem different. He tried to look ahead to getting back with his team. He did feel like he was letting the Cosmos down by not being there. He, also, felt like he was letting Sam down by leaving him for the team, no matter how much Joyce said otherwise. It was beyond conflicting.

Liz was great to Sam. She made him happy. She made him complete. She gave him everything he could have ever wanted in his life. Liz meant a lot to David because she meant a lot to Sam. Liz meant a lot to Joyce as well, another person that David loved so much. He felt like he was letting Joyce down by leaving as well. David felt bad because he couldn't think of a lot to look back on and be sad about for Liz. He couldn't understand if that was good or bad or neutral, if he was celebrating her life or mourning it; which one was right wasn't apparent. He did care for her; her quirkiness and her bubbly personality, but it was tough for him. It was like death wiped his memories of everything about her besides her death. David was sure his feelings would reach the surface eventually.

Stumbling and falling, he lands hard on his torso. He scrambles up to his knees and tries to get back up, but he realizes he's been caught. He looks at the ground underneath him. It's all black and slowly he starts sinking into it, like quicksand. The black envelopes him, he is cast into nothingness. The black turns to blinding white.

He can't see and his mind is swirling. He feels someone, or something, grab his hand. He can't see the hand, he can only feel it. A voice comes from the same location of the hand, at least he thinks. It has an echo and a reverb. "Come with me, we have work to do."

March 2nd, 2013

Joyce goes to her pocket, a week removed from the death of Liz, and pulls out her phone, expecting, or maybe just hoping, to see a message of any kind from her, through any service.

There was nothing.

Joyce had been spotty at work; some days she's there, some days she's not. Even when she was, was she really?

Joyce didn't have David here; duty resumed for him with the Cosmos. She was left to fall into her own circles of suppressed despair, even though she tried to remain hopeful. The hope did not come so easily for her internally. Maybe this was normal for death.

Another life gone, so suddenly and without good reason. Through David and through Sam, Liz had become her closest friend. They bonded mostly over movies and TV and other nerdy things. It wasn't that much different from her bonds with David and Sam, but it was different in some way. Joyce did not have many female friends, but by happenstance and right timing, she met Liz.

She was just great company for Joyce, especially when they grabbed lunch together at the mall during long days for each of them. Liz would never get angry. She was always a warm and kind presence and often giddy; she was never without a smile and never with a care. Another bright light extinguished.

Joyce took solace in the fact that she was onto the next life. A new kingdom, a brave new world ahead for her. She was not suffering anymore, at any point in time now. She breathed new life in new flesh. Liz was happy again, but how could Joyce be happy as well?

———————————

David watched Akio Ito pitch, continuing to monitor the situation with his arm. He had just returned to Florida after the funeral and personal time to man the baseball operations again, but he found it difficult to focus. The field used to provide bliss for him, but the now growing hole in his heart seemed to envelope any warm feeling he could muster, like a chasm opened up inside of his chest. David figured going headlong back into work was the only way to deal with this and move on.

He might have been wrong.

David pulled his phone out again and he found nothing in return from Sam. He sent him multiple texts and called him various times; all of the calls were missed, and that was probably on purpose. David couldn't blame him, because he couldn't imagine what Sam must be going through. David just wished he wouldn't close off entirely, especially with him. He knew it wasn't healthy, and some part of him thinks Sam knows that, too, but unfortunately Sam couldn't tear down his walls quite yet.

David would keep at it while keeping his feelings to himself. David definitely missed Liz now, after the shock of the funeral wore off, despite the noise on the field around him. She made Sam so happy, as she did everyone else around her. David's mind drifted to Liz calling him and Sam 'nerds' at the New Year's Party and it made him laugh as much it made him sad.

There was no reason for this to happen, David thought. It was so random and it made everything feel incredibly bleak. There seemed to be something bubbling inside of him, some anger, something hidden he couldn't quite realize in his mind's eye yet.

David was angry at something and nothing at the same time. A higher form putting him and his friends through such misery. That's where his mind always seemed to go: despair and rage while worrying about others and not himself.

David was scatterbrained; his mind seemed to leap from possibility to possibility. Was there a purpose to this? Was there a reason for this to happen? Some greater being teaching him… something? It seemed psychotic to him that death would be a teaching moment. Surely, there was some other way to learn whatever lesson that might be had.

Here David was, absentmindedly watching the team he was supposed to be leading. Barely there, only present in the physical state. David felt bad that he wasn't that strong of a leader at this moment, but he hoped everyone understood.

What could David do if the world of baseball couldn't bring him out of the black waters?

Then, David went back to Sam. David could not continue to focus on himself while his best friend was suffering. His world did not matter nearly as much as his right now.

David pulled out his phone again. He texted Joyce to try and check on Sam. David insisted on her going to see him, even if he didn't respond. David knew Sam needed someone. He felt guilty it wasn't him.

David felt horrible for not being there in Sam's time of need. The anger directed inward now. It was a palpable force.

Sam finally summoned up the courage to get out of his house. He looked back at the gray, two-story home, accented by white. This home was vacant and a constant nagging reminder that Liz was gone. Everywhere that she wasn't proved that their home became a house. It wasn't their home anymore. It wasn't his home anymore. It was just there. It just existed. The sadness would never leave this house. Nothingness permeated.

Sam opened the door of his small hybrid and sat down; he looked to the passenger side of the vehicle and a memory flickered, taking him back to a moment in time.

"Smile!" Liz exclaimed, seated on the passenger seat, as she had her phone pointed in his direction, in selfie mode. They were on their way to the local comic-con to promote their new book, Armageddon.

That photo immediately went onto social media, which he loved, but almost never said that. It wasn't a 'man' thing to enjoy being in pictures, which was stupid but felt innate; he had just wished he at least expressed how much it meant to him to Liz during their time. Sam loved the fact that Liz was proud to have him in his life. Little things like that were forever gone.

The memory weighed heavy inside his mind. Sam placed his hand on the seat next to him; he turned his gaze away from the seat and shut his eyes. Tears welled, but he pushed them back.

Sam knew she wasn't there, as much as he wished that wasn't true. She was gone. Forever.

Sam pulled into the parking lot of the mall, which had just reopened after being shut down for a week due to the fire, to see what was left of Comics Planet.

It was a skeleton of what once was. Caved in and charred by the inferno, in a state of complete disrepair (it was closed off enough for the rest of the mall to run like normal). He found himself walking into the store; he felt the soft crunch and release of the ashes of the books underneath him. There was nothing left. Sam morbidly thought Liz would have appreciated the metaphor of the store as the writer of the duo.

Sam turned around to leave the store and saw Joyce standing there just outside the wreckage; she must have been on her way to her own store. "Hey,"

Joyce waved timidly, "I went over to your place and saw you leave for here. Sorry to stalk and surprise you." She smiled half-heartedly.

"It's okay." Sam responded flatly. He guessed Joyce wasn't here for work then.

"How are you doing?" She paused briefly. "I know that's an impossible question, but I want you to know I'm here."

"It's getting better, I think." Sam didn't completely believe his own words.

"Well, that's good to hear." A silence fell over them for a minute. "Are you doing anything later tonight? I'd love to hang out and do whatever. Reminisce a little." It would help her as much as it would him.

"No, sorry." Sam made eye contact and immediately looked down to the pavement again. "I have something to do tonight." He paused. "I'm gonna start drawing again."

"That could be very cathartic. I don't want to interrupt that." Joyce smiled, but could clearly tell the conversation was nearing its end. The conversation was already on life support when it started, so she knew not to push it now. "Well, text me a picture of whatever you end up doing. Don't be a stranger." She smiled and left Sam.

Sam got into his car shortly after Joyce did and the day rapidly turned into night; he didn't know what happened to it. He gazed to his left and found a house. Sam was supposed to be here for the party and he was right on time, with twilight descending on his car, but he couldn't remember for the life of him when he drove here.

Sam lied to Joyce about starting to draw again. He just didn't want her to worry.

Sam was texted by an old friend, an old flame to be specific. The timing still seemed off putting to him. He felt guilty for it being so soon after Liz died, but he didn't plan anything with her in that way to begin with.

She asked him to come over, saying it would "help clear his mind." That's what he was hoping for.

She greeted him as he came to the door and immediately hugged Sam. "Sorry for your loss, honey."

"Thank you, Janice." Janice was a mixed woman, with curly brown hair down to her shoulders. Sam always did like her presence.

The rest of the night was mostly a blur for Sam; he still felt lost and aimless. Parties were not his element, unless it was with good friends, like David, Joyce, and especially Liz, which made him sad to think about. Sam stood in the corner of the room most of the night with a red solo cup that was bone dry for hours.

Sam remembered greeting his old friend again at the door, while meeting her new boyfriend, Max.

Max was somewhat obnoxious and pressing in Sam's eyes and didn't seem to want to leave anyone be.

Including now.

"Gonna join the party sometime?" Max asked.

"Huh?" Sam responded, getting pulled out of his haze. "Oh, um, yeah, I guess. I don't know."

"Here. This will make the night better." Max motioned his head for Sam to look at his hand.

A syringe.

Sam was taken aback.

"No, no," Sam laughed uncomfortably and made a dismissive gesture. "I can't do that."

"Why not?"

"It's just… not good." Sam felt quickly uncomfortable.

Max saw the unease and relented, but only a little bit. "Sorry, I didn't mean to put you into an awkward spot. It is highly addictive, I get it, but honestly," Max leaned closer "usage infrequently will not make it that way. It's a great feeling, truly, and if you hate it, just stop. Using it infrequently means you won't get addicted. Janice said you had a lot on your mind and she invited you to help you clear it. Not sulk. Try it once. It can make it all go away."

Sam knew that Max found out through his former girlfriend what was going on internally. Sam was at the point of no return; it was worth a shot, right? Now being convinced with Max's logic, he nodded his head.

Max wrapped a tourniquet around his arm, found a vein, and the injection was the least painful Sam had ever received. Immediately, Sam harkened back to the conversation at the party, how David talked about the degenerate culture of drugs in society. He was letting him down now. It compounded inside of him.

After it was fully injected, Max took off the tourniquet and implored him to take a seat, which Sam did.

Warmth took over and everything else that was bad was lost and forgotten. Sam hadn't felt this way since Liz's death.

The initial twenty minute rush was good. Very good, in fact. The next seven hours he sat there in a state of heightened wellbeing. Sam was very calm, relaxed, free of all pain and worry, weightless…

April 1st, 2013

The woman pulls him to his feet. She's older, probably twice in age. The woman's hair is long and luxurious and dyed black, with most of the dye faded to reveal a silver. She grabs his hand and leads him… somewhere. Where he was going was a mystery to him.

She shows him a memory. His memory, right? He doesn't know. They stand outside the vision, for him, by him. He's showing something to his family, but he can't place what exactly. Inside the reverie, the soft noise in the backdrop rapidly turns into a shout. The noise grows louder and he's swallowed by it. The world shatters around him at the realization of him not being cared for. In fact, he was never cared for, at any moment. He is lost.

He falls into her bosom, crying while simultaneously holding back. Words cannot or will not form, so he settles for the embrace. He can't reveal himself completely, not yet. There is no sound and no light in the room they occupy. The vision fades…

David woke up and, as usual, checked his phone. He was still worried about Sam, and the absence of messaging was not out of the ordinary for him as of late, but he still worried about him immensely. Joyce was able to see Sam once, to David's knowledge, so that was something, at least. Joyce said that Sam was drawing again and she hoped that would help Sam relieve some of his grief; David hoped so, too. He hoped that there were more times Joyce visited him, so Sam could stay afloat. David cursed baseball sometimes that he had to rely on Joyce to help his best friend.

He tried to call and message again as he awoke, but to no avail, like normal. David even tried to ask about his art as opposed to asking about his grief, in hopes that he could break the seal. Would Sam ever respond? David resigned to leaving him be for now, even though he didn't want to.

He opened his browser and saw the front page news which was another shooting. This one was at a concert. How could these people do such awful things? David thought to himself. It was heinous. People go to concerts to escape reality, to enjoy watching their favorite bands play their favorite songs, but instead were forced to live in infamy, as statistics to a world that didn't care after a day. These shootings seemed like they were happening daily anymore, and they were happening at more places than just concerts. The shooter was stated to have taken their own life after the fact. In David's eyes, the shooter deserved to rot in jail for what they did. Jail didn't seem to help, though, since many of the shooters took their lives inside of prison after the various massacres.

The school shootings were plentiful and seemed much more frequent than concerts, at least nine to one. That was sad to David. He couldn't understand and he didn't want to understand how someone could do such a thing.

The people responding to the incidents online had a day to see who could shout their opinions the loudest on social media and it eventually dissipated and everyone forgot. Then they would sit on their hands, do nothing, and wait for the next tragedy and do it all over again.

At schools themselves, there were also an alarming amount of children commiting suicide over bullying and cyberbullying. David couldn't help but open the comments on these posts and see the comments; they said that the kids should have thicker skin or learn to fight back. They shouldn't have to fight back at a place of education. Kids were being tortured by their peers for being different and not fitting in with cliques. Being different was a sin, it seemed. The widespread suicide and madness the world was seeing was only continuing,

Putrid. It was the only word he could think of to describe the world he saw around him, a world that was hurtling towards total cacophony. It was probably already there.

As awful (or ironic) as it might sound, he couldn't dwell on the madness of the world. It was time for his solace, because tonight was Opening Night and he was prepared to take the Paramount Baseball League, PBL, by storm. It was, in some ways, the only thing he could offer the world right now.

The Cosmos had the afternoon game and it could have been a better day overall. The seemingly endless winter held on for dear life as a cold, steady rain came down on both of the teams, but it was no matter as both teams finished the game with no delays. It was no matter to David, personally, either. Why? Because baseball was back until October. It was one of the greatest feelings you could have, according to David. This helped ease the pain of Sam closing off the past month and a half, the lingering torture of Liz's death, and the crazed world around him.

This game took place in the Cosmos' home, Megalopolis Bank Park. The park was fairly new; it just recently finished construction in 2009, only four years ago. What was even newer this year were the dimensions of the outfield walls. They were too far in distance from the plate and too high in relation to height. The pitchers loved being here, but batting was at an all-time low. Now, batters had a better shot of doing damage against opposing pitchers.

David wasn't sure how he felt about it. He thought that the batters should just improve as hitters, but he saw the merit of it from a fan's standpoint. Either way, David was ready to see his stud pitching staff take the field and, namely, his Japanese sensation today. David thought the pitching staff could definitely keep the opposing teams in the ballpark, even with the new dimensions. Akio Ito would get the nod to pitch for Cold Creek while Eddie Vulcano would get the nod for the visiting San Jose Dolphins.

His worry still remained during warmups; Ito's arm did not show any signs of regression, or progression, for that matter, but it still made him sweat. David was the one who denied the MRI, since he trusted his mens' instincts, so he let Akio Ito do his thing, but that put the pressure on him and him alone. At the end of the day, there were expectations on him and the team and seats to fill to watch them and bigtime names like Ito.

David was impressed by his team, but not surprised. They won, by a lot. The final score was 11-2, which kept their fantastic Opening Night record, the best in the history of PBL, in the win column for another year, although it was not without its drama.

Akio Ito left after four and two/thirds innings pitched, holding the problem arm by the elbow. He would be taken for an MRI to see if there was any structural damage. David crossed his fingers.

April 6th, 2013

The test results came back a couple of days ago for Akio, and they were not good. It was a complete UCL tear which means that he would have to undergo Johnny Tom surgery, effectively missing the rest of this season and potentially having to miss part of next year as well.

The signing was widely being speculated as the worst in the Cold Creek Cosmos' history online by the fans. The chatter from the devotees of Cold Creek would've taken the crown for the most ridicule the team received, if it weren't for the article posted today by CCS, Cold Creek Sports, a conglomerate news site for all of the city's sports teams. The article stated that Cosmos management knew beforehand about the injury, but pushed ahead with him anyways. It wasn't wrong by any stretch, pretty much accurate, honestly, but the responses were horrid.

The attacks were launched at Cosmos management, especially at the new GM, David, and the training staff for the poor signing, not vetting the talent for any prior injuries before they put pen to paper, and their poor decision making when it came to playing Akio instead of getting an MRI sooner and resting him. David only hoped it would come to pass and the team would begin winning even without the Japanese sensation. He was optimistic that winning baseball games, with or without the Japanese sensation, would cleanse the bad taste from the fans' and reporters' mouths.

He normally didn't let this stuff get to him, because he had dealt with vitriol before in his rise to this position. David had lived in the limelight, so he should be used to it, but he was human too. For one reason or another, this was getting to him and he couldn't shake it. He would have to compartmentalize.

"Tell it." the woman states matter-of-factly. She seemed to vanish in front of him, living in the periphery of his vision.

This was brand new territory.

These were uncharted waters.

He faced himself.

Only, what he faced was completely different from himself physically. He could still tell that what was before him was himself, in some way. It was something akin to a symbiote, vile tendrils oozing on the floor below them.

The symbiote began stretching itself over his body, consuming him. He wanted to fight it off, but the woman reentered the fray, seemingly out of thin air, in a dissipating circle around the frame.

"Don't." She was flat in her tone, like it was all business to her.

Black and red entwined with him. It seemed to be gleaning something from him. The symbiote retracted and turned into a mirror image of himself.

Now he stared at himself in full effect.

"Stop protecting me," he shouts. But why? What made him say that? "I need to go, be free, and move on."

"Who will protect you when I'm gone?" The mirror image spits back.

"You can." His voice becomes softer. "I want you to take on a new job. No more viciousness. No more contempt." He paused. "I know you're tired."

The symbiote looked softer. Like a burden being lifted off of his shoulders. The weight was now gone. "I am."

"Do you accept?"

"Of course I do." The symbiote says back, as if the answer was obvious, and begins to weep. The mirror image dissipates, the symbiote resumes its undulating form, and goes back to the room from whence it came.

Was that room always there? His thoughts are interrupted as the older lady grabs his hand.

"We're close." She says. They begin to float away…

———————————

Sam sat on his couch, with a painter's brush in his left hand and a syringe in his right, completely lost to the world. The TV was turned off, and yet his stare was affixed to the pictureless and soundless screen. Sam was a stone, not sure what he had to live for.

Sam's life was completely devoid of meaning, he hated everything and everyone, including himself.

He just couldn't wrap his head around Liz's death and he saw no way of returning from it.

Another day (or night?), another dark trip. Sam was chasing the dragon once again. Sam unraveled the tourniquet from his right arm and rested it on the table. He looked at the brush in his left hand and forgot that he even grabbed it. The only other things on the glass coffee table were an empty glass of days old… something and a razor blade.

Sam picked up the razor blade and looked at it longingly. As he came down from his high, he contemplated, like he always does, the thought of ending his life with the serrated steel. The turmoil he felt perpetually was very rapidly overtaking his life. If it hadn't taken over his life completely already.

How could he face anything in this life after what he had become? No one could save him. No man. No woman. No god.

He had no one to come home to. Nothing.

Yet, he couldn't go through with it. He thought about the pain that would be left in his wake. He realized how selfish he felt that was; another thing David said at New Year's. No escape from the living because of his guilt and no escape from the hell on this earth because of Liz's death.

Sam wanted something to take him from the land of the living and not make him do it himself. It would be easier for everyone. Sam hoped the dragon would leave scorched earth…

May 23rd, 2013

The voice kept calling and haunting Sam. "You're better off dead." That voice called to him over the past few months. It was the only voice he couldn't leave on read.

The inner voice kept beckoning him to end it. "This world is better off without you." Through the course of all this loss, his life continued to deteriorate around him. Sam's electricity shut off inside his house, as a result of not paying his bills, the trash piled up around him, and there were weeks-old dishes piled up on the table before him. His couch was imprinted by him, like something out of a cartoon. He had no will and was basically dead already. "You have nothing and no one left."

It was very early in the morning. One or two in the morning, to be exact, but Sam didn't bother to confirm it. It all felt like one never-ending night to him anymore. He felt like a waste on his couch. "You are worthless."

The syringe was lying on the table again. The injection would be far more than one human being could take. Sam knew that, and he didn't care. That was kind of the point. This was the end. He was glad this would take the pain away completely. A suicide without pulling the trigger. They would label it as a death by overdose, so everyone could sleep a little easier.

Sam picked up his phone and called David for the first time in months. David didn't answer; Sam wasn't mad about that. In fact, that's what he hoped for. He left David a message.

Sam picked up the syringe; he was staring at his end. He regretted doing this on David's birthday, but he couldn't live another day. Sam viewed this as a gift to him; David didn't have to deal with his lifeless husk anymore and could move on with his life. At least, that's how he comforted himself.

He plunged the syringe down into his veins. After injecting, Sam immediately regretted it. He knew it was wrong, yet there was no turning back.

It was a bittersweet symphony. The pull from the other side latched onto him and gave no release. His pain was ending, his misery receding, a pulse weakening…

It was almost three months removed, and while the shock had worn off, the pain remained for Joyce. It started to loosen its grip and that helped her at least face the days.

She was driving to Sam's place today; Joyce had made it a habit to see him at least once a week to check up on him and just talk, even though she mostly did all of the talking. Joyce liked to think it helped him in some way.

Sam had hardened up even more recently. He wasn't equipped to deal with it on his own, but who can really? She just wished he could convey it to her instead of shutting down entirely. Or to David. Anybody. Joyce provided as much space as she reasonably could without feeling guilt.

She feared for the worst every time she went to his house, with the dishes and trash piling up. Joyce knew he hadn't actually been drawing; she asked every time and Sam showed her nothing. The question was what exactly he was doing. The potential answers terrified Joyce.

Joyce arrived at their-er-Sam's house. Before she left her car, she sent David a birthday message: "Happy birthday, hunny. Wish you were here to celebrate. Win the game today ;)" She took stock of the time after sending the message: 9:48 AM. She had about an hour before she had to leave for work.

She left the car and rapped on the door; there was no answer. She waited a minute and knocked once more. Still nothing. She still had a spare key to the place, given to her by Liz to use for emergencies, so she used it and opened the door.

She tried the lights, but they weren't working. Joyce pulled out her phone again and turned on the flashlight and horror overtook her field of vision immediately.

Sam's lifeless body lay slack on the couch. Something she had feared was coming, but never expected. She didn't want to believe it, and yet all the evidence of belief was there. Joyce collapsed to the floor, mouth agape, in ever resistant disbelief.

In her haze, she managed to call 911, even though she didn't remember it. It felt like hours since she arrived there.

Joyce phoned David as Sam was rolled out in a black bag.

He buried the ax deep into his collarbone and blood instantly poured onto the wooden boat below them. He recognized the face of the man currently dying before him: it was his brother. He defected from his heritage and had this coming, but he couldn't help feeling pain, a crippling emptiness. He had it coming, he kept telling himself, but he felt terribly alone on this floating wood across the river. He began to weep for his brother…

The phone buzzed and David scrambled hazily to pick it up. It was past dawn and he gathered it was morning. 10:36 AM, to be precise; he probably should have been up by now anyways.

It was Joyce.

"Hey…" Joyce said, and trailed off. David felt like there was more to say.

"Hi..." David responded, very confused, "what's going on? Everything okay?"

"It's Sam…"

David's heart dropped.

"Sam overdosed this morning around 12 or 1 AM." The words were now falling out of her mouth. "He's gone. I had no idea… I should have known… I should have done something…" Joyce could not fight back the tears.

"It's not your fault…" David tried to comfort her, even through his own feelings. The shock overtook them both completely now; neither of them hung up, but they totally forgot about the call at hand.

David couldn't believe it; he had no idea he had fallen to drugs. Apparently it was heroin; Joyce had mentioned that at some point after she had said that Sam was gone, he couldn't remember when exactly. He kept his secret of hard times to himself and took it to the grave. The world was numb around David.

At some point during those glacial minutes, the call between David and Joyce was completed. He stared at the screen before him before he realized he had a missed call from Sam right before he passed. How could he have not answered? Damn sleep and damn these dreams making him so lost to the world during the night. David was furious with himself. He could have spoken to his friend for the first time in months. He could have spoken to him and talked him off of the ledge. He could have saved him.

He saw that Sam left a voicemail. "I'm sorry, Davey, for… for everything. Forgive me. Happy birthday. I love you." The shock was gone. David began to weep.

May 26th, 2013

The Cosmos granted David more time off for Sam's funeral today. It was three days after his death and David still felt numb; the world without him still made no sense.

David stood with Joyce, her arm wrapped around his, in the line waiting to say final goodbyes to Sam inside the open casket. The last ones before them completed their farewells and then David and Joyce walked to the cask. David attempted to crane his head upward to the sight of Sam laying there. It was horrible; this was the last time he would ever see him and it was as a lifeless cadaver. It would forever be ingrained into his mind. This was not how he wanted his last meeting to be and he couldn't fathom why anyone would want their last meeting with someone to be like this. He was rapidly overcome by an anger at the world he now found himself in.

The funeral was more of the same feelings he felt at Liz's funeral: a priest preaching religious garbage while seemingly forgetting there was a life lost and what the day was actually about. The proceedings were all a blur of anger and sadness.

David was now stuck in the same spot Sam was after Liz died: he had prepared a eulogy, but he never spoke it, even with Joyce persisting. He finally understood what Sam was going through that day. He wished he never understood that.

David was still mostly angry. How could Sam do this to them? He knew he was in pain, but to do this, he just could not understand it. How could he leave a wake behind him for all of us to suffer through? David quashed those feelings quickly, though. He knew they were unfair to Sam. Sam was suffering mightily.

He got angry at himself for not being there for Sam either. He blamed himself for this death; this could have been avoided if he tried harder to save him. If he wasn't with his damn team. If he was just there to pick up the phone.

David went on his phone after the funeral in the moments he could work up the strength to try and forget the agony he lived in, but that only made it worse. The posts he saw from everyone about his death on social media following contributed to his agony. They were wordless nothings and platitudes that meant very little; they were just 'look at me' posts instead of caring about the man that passed.

All he was offered by 'friends' and 'family' were thoughts and prayers (prayers to a God that just killed David's two dear friends off, with no purpose at all), with no one actually doing a damn thing to help. No shoulder to cry on, no one to talk to, just abject nothingness. They didn't seem to understand where David came from and thought those cliches were the cure all, even though all they did was look out for their own salvation and walk away, feeling better about themselves while the main party still suffers.

Even worse were the people who showed no sympathy for the dead. They blamed Sam and Sam alone for his death, which is why David quashed his earlier feelings of blame; seeing how others sounded made it sound completely ridiculous to him. They said he had it coming. He made the terrible decision and paid for it. It was awful.

David looked back at something Joyce said way back when. That there was more untold, that people deal with pain differently, that it was bubbling for some time. These people had no idea the grief Sam felt or the world he tried to cope with. They just hung onto their own ill-informed and ignorant opinions. A new view bestowed itself through this suffering.

Did I deserve this? David's thoughts drifted back to his own self-destruction. For something, anything, he said before that was wrong. For some crime he committed and didn't know about. For some sort of penance. Some morbid game of karma. Was it the argument they had during their last get together? Or was it the fact that he wasn't there for him, selfishly living his own life and being away? Was there some God punishing him for his wrongdoings, his shortcomings, his deficiencies? Or was it to make him better? Surely, there was a better way to make him a better person, for whatever crime he committed against this God.

May 23rd was David's birthday, when Sam died. David felt it was a cruel gift, some form of poetic justice. He should've been there more for him. He should've been more kind. He should've known better. He blamed himself. For everything.

David's leave from duty ended Monday. It was closing in on that morning, 9:30 PM to be exact. He was never much of a drinker, besides doing so, or used to do, rather, on their weekly game nights, but tonight he felt the need to drown his sorrows, to help him sleep better. So did Joyce as well. Long day. Long week. Long months.

Their beers came, to which Joyce raised hers.

"To Sam," she toasted, trying to be the light in David's life, "and to Liz as well." David absentmindedly clinked the bottles; he didn't even look up.

"You know what was my favorite memory of Sam?" Joyce said to David. He grunted in return. David guessed he had to pay attention. The anger and a new indifference was building and awakening underneath him.

"When he finally got signed into GD and began Investigator Comics." She continued after seeing no real response out of David. "I was never there when he created his first story, but I remember how happy he was when he got signed on to one of the big two. Sam was always a fan of that lore and then he finally got to write it." Stories he'll never be able to write again, David thought. Stories that can be cast to flame and be forgotten about for eternity. Like Sam was never here.

"Don't worry," Joyce consoled. David had trailed off from her reverie and she apparently noticed it. "They're just on to the next life. They're never really gone."

Bullshit, he thought to himself. More words that meant nothing to him and provided no solace from the noise in his head.

David never fully aligned with anything in terms of creed, an afterlife, or reincarnation, but that's all he could think about in this new wake. It didn't help that that was all that people offered him currently. No one knew what happened after, for sure, and neither did he; it just made him all the more angry.

David didn't know what to say in return, or rather how to formulate his thoughts to her, so he feigned a smile and nodded.

The closeness of their deaths, the suddenness, and how they seemed wholly unnecessary ringed eternal inside of him.

David sat there angry, sad, thinking, and drinking, wallowing in his own misery and pain. Thinking, thinking, and thinking. Spiraling in his own labyrinth of tombs and concern. He was paralyzed by his own mind. A war within himself arose. He harvested the seeds of his dead to begin his descent into the everblack. The rest of the night, like today, was shrouded in numbness.

———————————

At some point, David entered the taxi with Joyce. When? He didn't know. How? Also no idea. But he was with Joyce who was trying to pull him out of the trance through her physical touch. A hand on his hand the entire ride. David barely registered it.

David thought they had more drinks at home and then sauntered off to go home by way of taxi.

The next thing he registered, only barely, was the walk to the house. The time at the bar was a total blur, much like the rest of the week.

Then, they were in the house and quickly collapsed on the couch. Total exhaustion swept over them both. As they lay on the couch, the night ended abruptly with slumber.

An oversized, brown coat envelops him as he sits, legs on the chair, held against his chest.

"Your parents are dead…" The detective states as evenly as he can.

The words just told to him moments ago are the only thing he can find himself coming back to. The detective received no reply from the boy, so he gave him his coat and let him be. What could he be offered? His life was completely ripped to shreds, the fortress was collapsing and imploding in on itself. He was alone, completely by himself…

September 30th, 2013

The baseball season had come to pass and the Cold Creek Cosmos did not exceed, nor even meet, expectations. They finished with a dismal record of 70-92 after an injury plagued year.

David tried to go back to this organization like nothing had even happened, but his personal life infected his professional life. He could not escape the cell inside himself.

That did not stop the vitriol of the fans.

Many fans let him and players alike have it after a fifth consecutive losing season. The criticisms of him included the fact that he did not shop Roger Alden, the knuckleballer, after his Cy Young season to get players at other problem positions and future prospects. Alden turned in a mediocre earned run average of four plus and was a complete liability in the rotation. Now, his stock plummeted; no teams would trade anything of worth for him now. Akio Ito, of course, got injured in the first game and did not throw a pitch for the rest of the campaign and probably won't pitch for a good chunk of the next season either after getting Johnny Tom surgery; David faced the brunt of that as well. The fans thought he wasted money on the latter pitcher, especially after passing up on Alfred Gonzales who turned in a nice year, albeit on the offensive side, but a complete misuse of funds overall, and didn't get value for the former.

David buried that deep down inside himself as well as the general criticisms and even death threats thrown at him and the players across the season for underperforming and blowing season-changing and momentum-shifting moments during games.

The fans called for everyone's head and gave ill wishes to the players, the training staff, and the general manager, even extending the hate to their family members. They wished ill will on their metaphorical and unborn children, wished disease on the staff, and the players as well. '#DeathTo's became a dreadfully popular theme on social media for everyone involved. David felt that in his soul, if he believed in that anymore, even if this bile was mostly casted at his players. He was the brainchild of this entire operation. It was his fault they were even in that position in the first place.

The worst for David were the fans that thought he should get over the things in his personal life that were loudly affecting his work as the Cosmos general manager. David was silent about it all, though; he never mentioned it in any of his press conferences, talking only about the play on the field, and focused on his work, try as he may. David needed to 'leave his problems at home' and 'do his job,' and that he needed to 'get over it,' and 'stop being sad.' All of those criticisms were significant chunks being eaten off his already decaying life.

Back to the bottle, his sweet demoness. David couldn't express his thoughts with anyone, not even his fiancé, as illogical as that might seem from the outside looking in. He sent himself to his own exile. The cell walls were growing larger and more fortified. He couldn't let anyone else in. He couldn't be a bother to anyone else. He couldn't take anyone else down with him.

This was his fight and his alone. A fight that he was losing. Continual thoughts unrealized in his head. Why did he hate the funeral so much? Why did he hate everyone that was seemingly trying to help? Why did he hate?

David couldn't be normal ever again, or at least that's what he thought. This was all created by him. The guilt, the sadness, the anger, he was to blame for all of it. And he deserved it, he thought. The crown befit the kingdom.

It was drawing towards closing time at his now frequented location, Kenny's Pub, and he was hammered, all by himself. He didn't set up a designated driver for himself, nor a taxi; he would drive home on his own, because he didn't care. Nothing about himself he cared about or liked. David would drive himself through his own black haze, because no one could save him. Only himself, but he's even been failing at that. Just adding to his own weight.

———————————

The Final Era

After making it home despite his own deathwish, he sat in his car feeling the terror rise inside of himself. The dread, the void slowly swallowing him.

Breathing rapid. Panic throughout his entire frame. Nothing and no one to anchor him back. Hyperventilating. He wished he was dead, he's not good enough for this life, for anyone. The team was his fault. Sam's death was his fault. He's screwed every aspect of his life. It's all his fault. He wants to sleep forever. He wished something would take him so no one had to suffer anymore around him. So he didn't have to suffer any longer. No one cares about him. He's alone. He can't find his breath, he doesn't want to. Death is the only gift he could receive.

The aluminum meets the yarn-wrapped rubber and the ball is sent to right-center field, the ball rolls to the fence.

Unbeknownst to the young boy, the outfielders begin to disintegrate. He's focused; he continues to hustle, making sure to explode off the inside of the bag. The infielders begin to disintegrate into dust as he passes by each of them.

He touches home plate, looks to the stands, and everyone disintegrates before his eyes. Horrified, petrified, he turns around to see no one and nothing left. Everything is lost...

Daniel Drake

October 1st, 2013

David awoke after sleeping slack over the center console of the car. He wiped the drool off of his right cheek with his jacket sleeve and motioned to grab his phone. Twelve missed calls from Joyce. She had to have been worried out of her mind. How could he do this to her? It was all his fault.

After getting out of his car, he walked groggily to his house and opened the front door to see Joyce waiting and sitting at the head of the dining room table, with her head in her hands. He didn't expect to see her since it was 7:45 in the morning. She looked exhausted and it seemed like she didn't get an ounce of sleep. She looked like she had spent tears over him. It only added to his guilt. He deserved it.

As the door closed shut behind him, Joyce was startled out of her hands. There was a brief glimpse of happiness that registered over her face, before it was overtaken by anger. "Where in the hell have you been?" She was hysterical.

David gave no answer as his head sank, suppressing all of his emotions once again. He wanted to avoid this. He wanted to avoid her. She didn't deserve this unbecoming of him. She didn't deserve this decaying man deteriorating the relationship. She didn't deserve any of this.

He didn't offer a response as he made his way to the table in the kitchen and stood, leaning on it. He just didn't want to deal with this. He just wanted to sidestep the inevitable.

Joyce made her way out to the kitchen, becoming even more hysterical. She looked him in the eyes, or rather tried to, as David still held his head low. "All you do anymore is hide and drink and suffer. You need help." She was softer than she probably should have been.

"I'm fine." He said tightly. He wished he actually believed what he just said. The anger that he's felt for months coming up again, at her claims, and to nothing at all.

"You're not. Not even close." Joyce tried to keep her voice as flat as she could. "Where were you even at last night?"

David hesitated and deliberated far too much and Joyce took notice. "A friend's."

"Bullshit. You've shut yourself off from everything and everyone. You were drinking again, weren't you? By yourself. Alone."

By yourself. Alone. The words grate on David. Why? Was it the dreams? Was it because it was probably true and he wasn't ready for it? He wasn't sure, but it surely still pissed him off. An anger rising from the depths, from the void.

Joyce collected her breath and continued, "I love you from here to Mars and I don't want to see you like this." She wasn't sure what else to say. It seemed like nothing worked.

Grating, grating, grating.

"They were my friends, too." She continued, "I know what you're feeling here. This has been a terrible year, but these are the moments that define us…"

This trailed off, David wasn't paying attention. The only thing he wanted was for this to end. It was excruciating. She had no idea the pain he suffered from. These were all hollow words to him, words that made it about herself as opposed to the pain he was dealing with. She didn't have anything to offer him.

She slammed the table. "Are you even listening to me?"

The jarring of the table underneath him sent something rippling through his bones. He quickly found out what it was; he felt a queasiness in his stomach so he walked off to the bathroom. David threw up inside the toilet bowl.

She followed him and was saddened and disgusted with what she saw. "I love you with everything that I am, but you need to seek help. There's no shame in that," she trailed off, "you know damn well this isn't what Sam would've wanted."

Angered beyond belief. An anger that was starting to become him. He shot her a stare bound in stone. A glare that shot out a thousand daggers. "What he would've wanted?" His voice felt raw, as if it hadn't been used for millennia. "How the fuck would you know that? He's fucking dead." The words choked him as they came out.

David stormed off out of the front door of the house and got into his car.

He sat down in the driver's seat and began to shriek and shout complete nothingness. Wordless despair. Angry at himself, at the world around him, and at nothing at all.

David began to swing his fists at anything in his reach. He was slamming and smashing everything in his car and what was attached to it.

After his rampage, he felt his breath in staggered gasps. David looked in his rearview mirror; he was completely red in the face, with veins popping out, and he could see the residual rage that still remained.

David broke down at the sight of himself.

He started to sob uncontrollably into the steering wheel. He could find no release from the weight of the world crashing down on him. He was a waste.

Minutes had passed before David finally composed himself. He keyed the ignition and drove away from his house. He drove everywhere and nowhere. His house was a maze of memories. A reminder of how he was winning where losing was all. He had nothing and no one to go to.

He drove to a mall parking lot and sat in his car. The swirl of emotions he felt still radiated inside of him and he could not contain them any longer. He picked up where he left off and continued to cry. How much longer could he run?

———————

David decided on the bar. Kenny's again. He couldn't think of anywhere else. He ordered a draft, his usual.

"Nice Eliminator shirt." Said a random man behind him.

David turned and saw a man with frizzy, wild, and unkempt hair, almost like an afro, holding a beer in his left hand. He was a shade taller than David and rocked a flannel and ripped jeans. David grunted and returned to the beer. He forgot he was even wearing the shirt. How many days had he been wearing it?

"Sorry," the stranger continued, "just saw you walk in with it and thought-"

"Look, buddy," anger rising, "just leave me be." David paused and turned to face him. "Please." He stemmed the tide for now.

"I was bummed to hear about his passing," he persisted as if not hearing David; he sat down next to him, "he was great at what he did."

David gave in. "Yeah, he really was. I-I definitely m-" David trailed off, he couldn't even say it. He couldn't acknowledge he was gone, even after all of this time.

"You okay man?"

David did not respond. His head sunk, tears welling, with an anger about to come outward. He cooled off, pushed everything down, and brought his head slightly up.

The stranger sat on the seat next to him. "You know what my favorite part of Eliminator was?"

David didn't answer and took a swig from his glass, but it did not phase the stranger.

"His attention to detail for each panel. You know most times I read comics, I take the art for granted, but I took my time with that series. Each page I took in and got swallowed up by his world. I mean, just down to the most minute detail, the smallest person or thing." He continued to gush over Sam's art and David really couldn't blame him.

Everything he said was right. Sam was an incredibly talented artist. It brought a slight smile to David's face.

"There we go!" The stranger clasped his shoulder enthusiastically.

"I-um-I was…" David fumbled his words, but cleared his throat, "I was good friends with him. I actually met him after the fame and fortune."

"Really? That's amazing!"

"Yeah, we bonded almost instantly. You wanna know how the friendship was sealed?"

"How?"

"We were talking and I said the word, uh, 'word' in the whitest way I possibly could after something he said. He just bursted into laughter at that. It was the simplest, dumbest fucking thing."

"It always is."

"Yeah, when I first met him at a ballgame, I didn't even know who he was. No idea of how successful he was in that world. He definitely turned me onto nerd culture as a result of our friendship. I just talked with him like he was some guy and we became friends because of it, I think."

"I think so. People don't wanna get bombarded like that. Not to say having fans is bad and telling someone what their work means to them but still, it's probably tiring, right?"

"I agree." David knew all too well how damning the limelight could be.

David raised his beer and so did the stranger. Their glasses clinked. This was strangely cathartic for David.

"The name's Mark, by the way."

"David. Nice to meet ya."

They had a few more drinks and talked for a little while longer.

"...I was terrible at putting the story together, but I gave it my all. I wanted this elaborate proposal. I'm glad Sam and Liz were able to take my chicken shit and turn it into chicken salad."

"I bet." Mark said with a laugh. He looked down at his watch. "Oh shit, hey man, I gotta get going. Gotta get home to the girlfriend." He scribbled his number on a note. "Anytime you want to chat or come over, hit me up. Let's do this again sometime. It was a blast."

David nodded and said his thanks. "Hey." David called to Mark before he left. "Would you mind if I could crash for the night? I know it's weird to ask but there's some… friction at home right now." He felt awkward asking the question, but he didn't have much of a choice.

"Not a problem. Follow me."

Mark unlocked the door and it opened to a small apartment. There was a couch across the back wall and a TV across from it, situated on a stand in the crease where the walls met. A low coffee table that was too far out from the couch rounded out the room.

"This place is a shit show, I should've warned ya." Mark said.

David grunted and tried to say something, but it ended up being lost in his mumbles.

"We pay too much for too little, honestly, but it still gets the job done. The old lady is probably asleep already. But the couch is all yours. The remote is on the table. We have some shit on the smart TV. Have at it."

He laid on the couch, grabbed the controller to put something on, but before he knew it, he was out like a light.

The night was a smothering red, as if the night sky would leak lava.

The rubber of the tires was tearing across the pavement. He was driving quicker than he should and there was a sharp bend incoming. There's something on the road, a cat. His cat?

He sharply turns left and the car turns over on its hood.

He crawls out of the vehicle, with the world literally upside down. He saw that his evasive maneuver was too late. He hit the cat.

He makes his way over to the now deceased animal. He quickly realizes it was his cat. He picks up the limp carcass and begins to weep…

The Final Era

October 2nd, 2013

Karen groggily stumbled down the steps in the early morning, still in her PJs and oversized white T-shirt. At the bottom of the staircase, she turned the corner to find a body on the couch in the living room. She kept walking.

Wait, Karen thought to herself, what did she just see? She walked over to the couch and prodded the man and he jumped out of sleep. Karen leaped back and screamed.

"Who the hell are you? Why are you in my house?" Karen was blanched at the sight.

David was still in a haze, but tried to get it together as quickly as he could. "I-uh-I'm…" He fumbled the words.

Before he could fumble anymore, Mark came rushing down the stairs, appearing to have just woken up himself due to the ruckus. "I'm so sorry, Karen," he said, "this is my friend David. I thought I'd wake up before you honestly." Mark shrugged, with a grimace on his face.

"Jesus Christ." Karen was exasperated. It was far too early for her to be this exasperated.

"I'm sorry," David said, "I can just get out of your hair. I knew I shouldn't have imposed on you."

"No, no…" Karen paused and collected her thoughts for a second, "no, you're fine, honey. I'm just... startled is all. I was actually just about to make breakfast," she laughed to herself, "you want some?"

"If that's okay." David was already in position to leave. He felt out of place.

"Absolutely, dear." Karen seemed to realize David's apprehension and added, "I'm more than happy to. A friend of my Mark is a friend of mine."

Immediately, David was charmed by her. Those little pet names he enjoyed, even if it meant nothing at all. He loved her welcoming presence. He could see why Mark was with her.

David looked at his phone; more missed calls and texts from Joyce throughout the night. He was too afraid to face her so he left them for another time. He felt a lot of guilt for putting her through this and even more for procrastinating further on letting her know where he was.

"Sorry about that, buddy." Mark made his way fully down the steps after Karen went to the kitchen to prepare breakfast. "I should've texted her or something so she could have seen it when she got up."

"No worries, man. You put a roof over my head, I can't complain about a lack of sleep." David smiled at Mark.

"That's Karen, by the way." Mark and David shared a laugh. Mark sure knew how to make a situation light-hearted.

The TV was on. Apparently, David had at least turned the TV on last night before conking out. "Can you believe this?" Mark asked.

On the screen was the news; there was another mass shooting. David had been numbed to it, by this point, and that made him feel… something about himself. Was it the long year for him personally? Was it the fact that he had seen so much violence and sadness throughout the year that it didn't faze him anymore? He couldn't tell. "It's insane." That's all David could muster up.

David got distracted from the TV by the smell of eggs, sausage, and bacon being cooked; it sparked his appetite for the first time in a while. He hadn't even noticed it was gone until this moment.

They made their way to the table. "Want anything to drink?" Mark asked. "We have coffee, OJ, soda…"

"Sure, I'll have a coffee." David hadn't had coffee in a while. It was normally alcohol these days, so he was salivating for a cup of it.

Mark made a right towards the kitchen, just before the tiled portion of the room that had the table. "Do you want one, too?" He asked Karen as she finished up with the food. David heard her say yes.

David sat down at the table. The table was situated across from the counter with the sink. It was a small black table, with four steel padded chairs around it.

Karen and Mark joined him with cups of coffee and plates of food for everyone there, and then some.

"How did you sleep?" Karen asked as she handed the plate of food to David. "All considering." She added, with a smirk.

"Eh, I slept okay. I've always had difficulties with sleeping but…" He trailed off, wanting to speak about the bizarre dreams he's been having, but they didn't care about his unimportant dreams. "But it's gotten worse now."

"What do you mean, honey?" She was so sincere. David couldn't help but try and open up.

"I-uh-I'm not sure. It's just gotten worse." At the end of the day, David continued to restructure shells to keep them out.

"Well, eat up." Karen smiled. David finally took her in physical beauty after that. She had black hair, peppered with gray, and had a highlight of red that looked like it was on its way out.

They ate mostly in silence, besides giving praise to the well-cooked meal.

David left his phone on the table and it began to vibrate, disrupting the hushed meal. He ignored it, or at least tried to, but with two other people it was impossible to do so.

Mark and Karen looked at each other and then, after several buzzes, Mark said, "Go ahead and take it, man."

David sighed. "Something I'm not sure I wanna deal with right now, honestly." He gave an uneasy laugh.

"Whatever it is, you know you can't run from it forever." Karen stated.

"I know, but… I just don't know." David shrugged his shoulders.

Karen couldn't help but see his phone screen after the attempted call stopped.

"How many missed calls?" She exclaimed at the volume of them on his screen. "Joyce, huh? Who is Joyce and why are you avoiding her?" She got a real good look at this screen, David thought to himself.

David didn't answer, avoiding eye contact.

"Give her a call back, hon. Like I said before, you can't run forever."

"It's complex," David got defensive, "and I haven't really dealt with it the right way. Now, I feel like there is no right way to deal with it, so I just… haven't."

David felt like a complete dump after uttering the words. He was trying to justify his poor behavior. The poor behavior that was causing the friction in the first place and attempted justification was only making it worse. He just didn't want to face it. Guilt on top of guilt.

"I might be speaking out of my own element here, but I know death is... tricky, especially with a close friend." Mark paused. "But you can't run away from it forever. Like Karen said."

Karen chimed in. "Precisely. I don't know what exactly you're going through, but when my mom passed away years back, I shut off a little bit myself. I had no one to fall back on then. It was me against the world. I wish I would've had someone this worried about me." She gestured to the phone. "Please don't take it for granted."

David nodded without conviction. He knew they were both right. He knew he had to face it.

"Well, thank you for the meal." David got up from the chair. "But you're right. I have to go take care of this."

"I'm glad we could help." Karen said and Mark nodded in agreement with her.

David received a hug and a handshake from Karen and Mark, respectively, as he left their apartment. He shot Joyce a quick text, saying he was coming home and he would talk with her about everything.

———————————

David arrived back home. He felt more wanted by his house than he had in recent memory. Sending that small text lifted some of the weight from his shoulders.

He turned the key to unlock the front door and he walked to the living room. David found his fiancé sitting on their couch in an even worse catatonic state than previously. Guilt on top of guilt.

"I called you and I-I texted you and you-you didn't respond." She was a complete wreck, tears beginning to stream again on her raw face. She kept pleading and crying.

Head sunk, he walked over and plopped down next to her. David fell into her chest and began to sob.

"I'm so sorry… for everything…"

Joyce was a little taken aback and abated her tears for a moment. His admission of wrongdoing eased the pain she felt a little bit.

"Shh, it's fine." Joyce consoled. "We'll get you some help, okay?"

David knew she would do everything in her power to help him. He was so lucky to have her. That made him feel bad about himself; why did she have to take care of him so much when she was struggling mightily as well?

Either way, he was thankful for her. He couldn't believe he strung on an angel like her for so long.

Joyce was miraculously able to get a doctor's appointment for David the same day he came home to her.

"How are we doing today?" The female doctor asked, in a monotone, indifferent voice.

David immediately shut off after that; he didn't feel safe with her. Joyce noticed and took the lead.

"He's been going through some mental trauma for months now and we want to see what we can do. We think it might be depression."

The word 'depression' rang in David's head. Hearing it said out loud made him feel embarrassed but also relieved.

"Anything that caused it?"

"The death of two close friends."

David started to cry. Even the uttering of 'two close friends' was enough to sting him.

"I gotcha." The humdrum demeanor and dismissive tone annoyed David. "Well, I can prescribe you some medication. I will start you out with ten milligrams and see if that helps."

"Sounds great. Thank you so much."

After the doctor's appointment, they went to the pharmacy to pick up the prescription. David looked at the package and already did not want to take the medicine. It mentioned things about taking while pregnant or while being on your period, and it made David feel like less of a man. It was like being depressed wasn't a manly thing.

When they got home, David finally worked up the courage and took one of the pills. Surprisingly, he already felt a clear difference in his mind. A clarity he hadn't felt in a long time.

Maybe there were blue skies ahead.

The black and red symbiote walked with him towards the door. Why was he walking towards this door?

He opened the door to a blackened room, a complete absence of light permeated. He continued to walk inside the room with cautious steps. His instincts kicked in and he extended his foot and he felt water. Immediately, a light pulses, as if it was activated by his touch.

From the water, a shapeless, black blob ascends, akin to a void. He makes his way to the control panel and plunges the lever down. How did he know where this control panel was? "Thank you. And... I'm sorry." He says to the blob as he gets sucked down by the whirlpool he created.

He heads out of the room and sees his protector. When did she get here?

Daniel Drake

She embraces him, "I'm proud of you." She says. All three of them walk away and leave the room behind. They can finally leave it all behind.

Act II: "The Faint Pulse of Light"

Daniel Drake

The Final Era

October 13th, 2013

Perilous, suspended, floating in nothing. A black surrounds him. He can't move and he can't feel anything around him.

Was it death? Was he finally gone? It can't be. Or can it?

He could still see the… nothing that surrounded him, so he couldn't be dead, right? He couldn't do much of anything parlalyzed inside of this perpetual black.

He continued to search and it finally breeds purchase. A faint pulse of light at the end. Can he swim? Try as he may, he couldn't, but the light kept pulsing and taunting…

With the medication at work, David did feel an overall change in his everyday life. He dove back into his hobbies, mainly his love of nerd culture, which helped block out the remaining noise in his head.

He also fell back into managing his baseball team. David had given the reins to his assistant for the longest time, but he was ready to leap back into the world of baseball, with this year's Winter Summit fast approaching.

It felt good to be excited about something again.

The only thing that remained were his dreams. David didn't know what to think of them and kept them to himself. They were so lifelike, so far away from him, and yet so close. He would try to bring them up next time he goes to a doctor, although he was very afraid of what it could lead to. What if the doctor thought he was crazy? What if they sent him away to some wackjob compound? He wasn't crazy, David knew that, but that means nothing to a doctor. He was scared of that possibility so much that he would probably just keep the dreams to himself for a little while longer. David wanted to be normal again, though, so maybe the risk of telling the doctor was a calculated one. He would run it by Joyce beforehand. That's a good idea, he thought.

Either way, today was special for him for a couple of reasons: it was Mark's birthday and he would make the call to get back to work for the Cold Creek Cosmos.

David couldn't believe how far he had come within a week and a half; and neither could Joyce. Everything was starting to come back around for him. He found himself making goals and making plans again; it was great.

Joyce was with him today for Mark's party; it would be the first time Joyce met Mark and Karen. David was excited, since he attributed a lot of his comeback to them. It was important to him that Joyce met them.

"Hey!" Mark exclaimed as they made their way to his yard where they were having the cookout. "And you must be Joyce. Pleasure to meet you." Mark took her hand and shook it. The sensation sent a ripple through Joyce. There was something familiar about it.

"Yes. Nice to meet you as well." Joyce replied.

Karen came rushing up to them, seemingly out of nowhere. "Hello, I'm Karen." She hugged them both.

They walked into the house and noticed two people playing games on the TV. Mark noticed their glances.

"Ah yeah, sorry, this is Kyle and Tim." He motioned to the two in order. Kyle, the first one introduced, had blonde dreadlocks and was rail thin. Tim had short cropped black hair and an almost military look. They waved absentmindedly to David and Joyce before returning to their games. "We actually play music together."

"They're fantastic." Karen said.

"Ah." Mark brushed it off, evidently hating to be complimented, and then continued, "We play some psychedelic rock, but we try to keep an open mind for anything."

"What do you all play?" David asked.

"I'm the 'singer,'" Mark air-quoted jokingly, "and I play bass as well. Kyle here is the drummer and Tim is the guitarist." Mark paused and turned to David. "Do you play anything, man?" Karen and Joyce talked amongst themselves as they shuffled back to the yard.

"Well, I always liked messing around on my grandma's piano, but I was never too religious with it. I kind of regret it."

"Dude, that's awesome. I take it you don't have a keyboard?"

"Nah."

"Well, we'll have to go get ya one!"

"Really?"

"Hell yeah, man. Imagine all the sweet synths you could provide us." Mark said with a smirk. David smiled as well.

"Awesome." David thought about it some more momentarily, and then decided, "Yeah, I'm game."

More goals and more things to look forward to. David was getting better with every passing moment.

"Are more people coming?" David asked, anxious about the possibility of more strangers.

"No, we're good with what we're at now. I don't want a big thing."

"Why not?"

"Eh, birthdays just aren't a big deal to me anymore. The smaller the better."

David nodded. He could understand birthdays not meaning much anymore, after losing Sam. The peril, the grief, the sorrow. He still couldn't believe he was gone…

No, he thinks to himself, shut it out. It does no good.

"So what is the plan then?" David asked.

"Well, Karen got me this movie that I think you'd dig, so we're definitely gonna watch that. Probably cake, ya know. The works. Don't want to change the classics, right?"

And so the works came and went. They had dinner, presented the candlelit cake, with Kyle saying he 'smelled like one too' after the birthday song, and they watched the movie Karen had got for Mark.

David fell into the movie. He used to be a huge buff; doing reviews of them, annual rankings, rankings for each movie universe. It used to be so much fun for him. It would just be another thing to add to his hobby list.

He did notice something weird while watching the film, though: the flick had tremendous emotional weight and yet he felt very little of it. He felt like a robot and it felt… wrong that he couldn't appreciate the heartfelt story.

That would be something to figure out, if it didn't stop soon. David would bring both things up to Joyce. Eventually.

––––––––––––––––––––

"David! Glad to hear from you. How are you feeling?" The president of the Cosmos, Gaylord Moyer, asked.

"I'm getting better, I feel like everything is falling back into place again." David was happy to hear a familiar voice again. It felt like a piece of his family was returning to his life.

"Glad to hear it. Feeling better enough to come back to the team? Don't get me wrong, we've loved the work your assistant has done in your stead, but there's a reason we hired you." Straight to the point; David enjoyed that about him.

"That's actually exactly why I called. I would love to come back as soon as possible."

"We will happily reinstate you as soon as tomorrow, but," the team president continued, his voice growing slightly somber, "there's just one thing. The world knows what's been happening in your personal life. You can't keep a secret in the limelight. You have to be candid with our fanbase and the world for them to accept you back into the fold. It's an uphill battle, but we know you can handle this." He paused.

"That's why we hired you." David could feel the smile from the other end at his own clever repetition.

David knew what he meant and feared the worst, but Gaylord reassured him. "We still want you back. The fans want you back, even if they were vicious with you all year. This team needs its leader again."

"Thank you for the vote of confidence in me. It means a lot. I understand what I'm up against and I will do what is needed."

"Good." The president went on, "This is what is going to happen: we will make a press release announcing your reinstatement and it will include the date of the press conference officializing it. We will send you a private email of the time and place for it. We need an apology, even though these were circumstances out of your control. At this point, it doesn't really matter. And, finally, a promise to move onward and upward."

David heard him sigh through the phone before he continued, "Now the tough part, son. Any more slip-ups and we might have to move on from you for good. Understood?"

David knew this business was cutthroat and did not care about feelings. "Of course, sir." He accepted it for what it was.

"Great! We will get the process rolling."

"Thank you for bringing me back and thank you for your understanding through these trying times. You've been like a second family to me through all of this. I won't let you down, sir."

"Of course. Glad to have you back onboard."

With that, the call was done and David could get back to work. He was elated, and very nervous at the same time.

Climbing up a spiral staircase, which looked like a coil from a playground. The coil felt small and massive at the same time, as did he. The space of this world felt uneasy. He climbed, trepidatiously, to the top.

He's scared for his life, he wanted to jump but the fall was too great, even if it actually wasn't.

He descended to the ground below him, with his tail between his legs. There was a man waiting for him and he was disappointed in him. So was he…

October 16th, 2013

"…and without further ado, David Renninger."

The flash of cameras and small applause rained on him as he made his way behind the desk and into his seat. David shook the hands of the two presidents of the team, Gaylord and Preston Moyer, the team's coach, Joseph Crigel, and the team captain, Darin Ricketts.

David was obviously nervous about the imminent press conference. His nervous ticks were prevalent over the past few days: biting his nails, pacing; he was sure Joyce was sick of him by now.

What if they didn't take him back in? How big of a hole had he dug? Did he deserve any of this? David sometimes spiraled down into a darker place. He did his best to keep that at bay.

"I would like to start with an apology." David leaned forward into the mic as he spoke. "What I did to this team was inexcusable. Absolutely inexcusable. I am very sorry for the torment, embarrassment, and uncertainty I have caused to this great organization. An organization that I loved. An organization that I still love. I want the best for this franchise, and the best was not given throughout this past year."

"How do you plan to make amends for your actions?" A reporter asked.

"I plan to make amends by giving this team another fighting chance to progress onward and upward." He turned and smiled at Gaylord, who smiled back. David turned back to the crowd and went on, "I said it last year and I'll say it again: I want to win now, and in the future. Moreover, I will be speaking and helping out with organizations for mental illness and alcohol abuse, both of which I've suffered from and survived."

"With the transition back to the team, what are you going to do to win back the favor of your team and your fans?" Another reporter asked virtually the same question.

"The only way I can. I will keep going forward and helping in the Cold Creek community. I hope this will show how serious I am about this change for the better. It will not be easy and an apology is not enough. I will need to show that I can be a leader again. Someone they can trust and someone that the fans can trust. And I will do my best to accomplish that."

"After the disappointing last season, what's the plan with the team going forward?" A third reporter piped up.

Ah, back to baseball, no more talk of him. The worst part of this press conference was history, David thought.

"I will bring the best twenty-five players up north to Cold Creek this coming year. Whether it be from the players already on the team," David gestured to the captain, "young guns down in the farms, or free agent signings to make it the best twenty-five in the PBL, you have my guarantee." He paused and flashed a smile. "I said it in my inauguration: I've loved this team since I was a kid and I still do. My dream is to bring the World's Crown back to Cold Creek and I will do everything in my power to accomplish that."

The people behind the scenes were waving him off, signaling the end of the press conference.

David's eyes settled back on the reporters with their recorders. "I would like to say again how apologetic I am and how much I'm looking forward to the future of this team. With that, it's time to get back to work. Thank you."

With a nod, David and company left the podium and the press conference behind. He was as excited as he was nervous, but the possibilities were endless. He was ready to get back to work.

"Great work, Davey." The team presidents said in unison. It pinged something in David's memory. It reminded him of how Sam called him that. He still missed him…

"We're glad to have you back." The coach interrupted his thoughts.

"What they said." The team captain interjected and they all shared a laugh.

"Thank you all."

David felt a vibration from his phone. A message from another general manager from the league.

The message read: You have a deal.

David was so happy to be back.

Daniel Drake

He was back, suspended in the black, the light still taunting. He was paralyzed and couldn't swim. He tried and he tried but he failed…

He didn't recognize the older lady he once knew. He didn't want to see her like this. Was she stricken with something? He couldn't figure out if she was but he knew there was very little time for this woman he apparently knew.

Whatever the reason she was suffering for, it pained him to see her like this. She was barely the person he remembered her as. Something was defeating her and took over her mortal coil completely. Something he didn't know and something he loathed.

The pain was too great. He didn't want to see her like this. Separation was all he wanted. He just wanted to be alone…

October 18th, 2013

David was still on an intense high after the past two weeks. Not only had he gotten into a better state of mind, but he had gotten back to his old job. He would have to wait until the end of October to really get things going and the ball rolling (although, that didn't stop him from having a deal to trade players in place already), with the playoffs still going, but he was excited for the future regardless.

David couldn't thank the Cosmos organization enough for its kindness, generosity, and forgiveness. They had no reason to bring him back, with the embarrassment and off-field troubles he brought to the team. And yet, they still brought him back, proving how much of a family they are to him.

He also wouldn't be here without the love of his wife, Joyce. She stayed strong through the devastation, and gave him something to lean on, even when he didn't want it. Even when she was hurting as well. He almost certainly didn't deserve her, but he still couldn't believe how lucky he was.

"I have returned from the wiz palace." Joyce declared, jokingly. David laughed. It felt good to laugh.

They were out celebrating David's return to work. Joyce was beyond thrilled for him. It was a long road, but everything felt like it was back to normal.

It was perfect timing that Joyce came back just now, since their food had arrived two minutes after the fact. They ordered and were now presently eating lobster and other seafood. David wasn't terribly fond of it. It had nothing to do with the actual food and everything to do with the bill; it would probably make him see red later.

"How is it?" Joyce asked.

"It's good. Not thirty dollars good, but ya know." David joked.

Joyce laughed. "We didn't have to come here. It is supposed to be your day after all."

"Are you kidding? After everything that's happened, you deserve it. You love this place. I'm just happy to be anywhere with you." David grabbed her forearm and rubbed it with his thumb lovingly.

"So how's your fifty dollar lobster?" He asked with a grin.

"I love it. I might get seconds." She winked.

"Like hell you will." They both laughed.

The night rolled on. The laughter and good times continued, David was putting it off long enough, the dreams and the robotic nature of the medication, so he finally asked.

"Have I been… normal again to you?"

Joyce looked perplexed. "It seems like it to me, by all accounts." She paused. "Why do you ask?"

"Well, I love that the medicine is helping me out and making things easier but… I feel almost robotic since I've been on it."

"What do you mean?"

"The other night, for example, at Mark's party, we were watching that movie and there were some emotional parts and yet… I didn't really feel sad about it, even though I should've been. I didn't feel much of anything while watching it, to be perfectly candid. It just seemed weird to me."

Joyce pondered, but before she could speak, David continued,

"There's one more thing," David paused, fearing she'd think the worst, "I've been having these dreams. Super lifelike, surreal, almost like I've lived these moments before and yet I haven't all in one. Like I'm a spectator to some other life. Sometimes, it's like I'm a spectator to my own life."

Something sparked inside of Joyce's mind, but she couldn't place it. It felt like something wanted to come to the forefront, but couldn't, like it was being blocked out. Like the dreams meant something. "I hate to say I have nothing for you but, I have nothing for you here. This is definitely out of my range of knowledge." David felt defeated that she couldn't offer him anything here. "But it's definitely all important, though." The reassurance brought David's spirits back up. "I'll tell you what, we'll set up another appointment-"

"A new doctor," David interjected, almost automatic, without thinking, "please."

"Of course. You didn't like the other one?"

"No. Not at all."

"That's perfectly okay." Joyce assured him. "I'll get you set up with another."

"What would I do without you?" David smiled and gave her a kiss as he leaned over the table. He grabbed her hand.

"You'd probably be dead." Joyce laughed, but David thought of Sam. "Sorry. Sounded funnier in my head."

"It's fine. Anyways," he pointed to the ring, "we have to set a date. How does January 11th sound?"

Joyce said yes, with tears welling. January 11th was Liz's birthday and she loved that symbolism. She could celebrate her and her marriage simultaneously.

Another great day, David thought.

Bitter cold. Walking under a dead sky. The winds of winter were beating him relentlessly as he forged through the night. Where was he going? Why did this feel so real? He stood outside of this dream, yet in it as well. Again. He had to take over, yet lacked the strength to do so.

The winter did not forgive but he kept moving automatically. Where was he walking to? Why did it matter this much? All questions went unanswered but only because he already somehow knew them and did not all the same.

He continued through this bitter path to nowhere. He would find the key to nothing and everything all by himself...

The Final Era

October 21st, 2013

David was looking at his phone. It was on the news app (he had somehow gotten there after checking on the postseason of baseball) that came pre-programmed into his phone and he saw yet another school shooting. More children slaughtered for no reason at all.

He logically understood again why this was objectively sad, but he still didn't feel much about it. David couldn't tell whether it was the numbness to the mad world he lived in or if it had to do with the medication now. Good thing he was at the doctor's now.

The doctor opened the door and interrupted his train of thought as she sat down in front of him. She had graying blonde hair and was of average weight and height. "So what can we do for ya?"

David sat on the weird bed with the weird piece of paper. This was the new doctor Joyce set up for him; her name was Valerie, and she was already much brighter and cheerful than the doctor who first prescribed him. Joyce found her through Karen, who only had great things to say about her. David could see why Karen loved her; the resemblance between their personalities was uncanny. It was almost like this was Karen 2.0.

David was alone today. No Joyce by his side at the doctor's office. "This medication I'm on…" he stumbled over the words, making sure he found the right ones, "it makes me… it makes me feel… robotic."

"Hmm, well our chemical makeups are different from person to person. No one medication works for everyone. Lemme see what we can start you up with next." She sealed it with a wink. David was much happier with this doctor.

The doctor prescribed him with a new medication and told him to ween off the old medication by splitting the tablets in half and taking it every third day for the next month, while taking the new medication on every other day he didn't take the old one.

David almost told her about the dreams, but he kept them all to himself for a little while longer; he was honestly scared to share them and scared of them as a whole. He didn't know what the doctor would think and he didn't want to be sent to a looney bin for some disorder that he knew he didn't have. And, maybe, the new medication would help combat them, too, somehow. He kept it locked away for now.

The Final Era

October 22nd, 2013

He hit the keys on the synthesizer before him and pushed a lever on the side to make the sounds fluctuate and bend. David didn't know much about keyboards or pianos, but he knew that he liked to play them. Parts of it made sense to him, and that was more than he could say about any other instrument.

Nearby, he heard relentless smashing on the drums by Mark. It was completely incoherent; he wondered how much of a novice he actually was to music himself or if it was just his lack of skill on that particular instrument itself.

David was anxious about today; he wanted to come but he also didn't. He wanted to hang out with his friend, but he feared something would go wrong and that Mark would hate him and his playing ability. A battle inside of his mind still remained, but to a lesser degree.

As he turned back toward the synthesizer, Mark seemingly appeared behind him. "You like that one?" He startled David so much, he almost jumped.

"I do. I just don't know if I'm really set on it." For whatever reason, he just wanted an excuse out of this whole thing. Buying the instrument. Playing with Mark, Kyle, and Tim. He wanted to play with friends, but he was nervous about failing.

"Why not?"

"It's a little pricey." David grabbed the price tag to show Mark. Mark wasn't deterred.

"Oh, there's plenty of reasons not to get it. Money is nothing, it's a circle. It's given to you by someone, you spend it somewhere, and then it makes its way back to you. It means absolutely nothing. You can't take it to the grave, so why not spend it?"

"Fair point. Although, I probably should get an actual keyboard. A synthesizer is cool, but its uses aren't dynamic, like a keyboard. There's just so many options to choose from on a keyboard."

"True, true, I can understand that. I tried to play a little back then and I was able to get some mileage and new sounds out of it."

David nodded in agreement.

"I'm sure you've been hearing me." Mark motioned to the drum kit he was just recently thrashing. "I've been messing around with this kit. Just for fun and also to potentially piss off the workers." Mark snickered at his own joke.

David laughed but tried to bring the conversation back to what he was doing. It seemed like Mark didn't care all of the sudden. "This one looks good." David pointed to the keyboard he messed with before he drifted towards the synthesizer he was currently at.

"I was hoping you'd pick that one." Mark smiled. "It's the same one I used when I played before." David smiled at him.

"I'm probably gonna pick up some new picks and strings myself." Mark gestured vaguely behind him.

"Sweet."

David didn't understand why, but Mark's propensity to pull the conversation back to himself bothered him. He couldn't place why, but it did. He guessed what Mark had to say was more important than what he had to offer.

———————————

After they got done buying their things at the music store, David and Mark made their way back to Kyle's home, where they held practice. They didn't even bother with the front door and opted to go to the garage, which was attached to the house, so they could all jam together.

Kyle and Tim greeted them and David immediately recognized the medicinal smell that greeted him. Kyle passed the blunt around to Tim and then to Mark in stride. Mark motioned for him to smoke as well. David declined with a wave.

"You don't smoke?" Mark asked.

"Nah, never have." David replied.

"Why not?"

"Never saw a reason to."

"All good, man." Kyle said, motioning for the blunt to return.

"But you drink." Mark retorted, while not passing it to Kyle.

David's face became annoyed and Mark held up his hands as if to placate him. "Or rather, used to." Mark continued after a pause. "I'm just stating a fact that that stuff is so much worse for you. This," he held up the blunt, "helps out with a multitude of things and it doesn't have any addictive quality to it."

"He doesn't do it, no big deal." Tim interjected. "Stop preaching like this stuff like it's a godsend. You have no medical reasoning to do it. You just like to do it because you like being high." That received a nice laugh from Kyle and David. It was so much funnier to them since they knew it was the truth.

"Don't listen to them, I'm right, try it." Mark would not relent as he brandished the blunt once again to David. Mark made it about himself and his interests again. David was hoping it was just a bad day for him, but what did he know? Mark was probably right again in this situation. What Mark said was more important and more intelligent than what David thought.

David gave in with a shrug and tried it. He put his lips to brown paper and inhaled. A coughing fit erupted out of him.

"You alright, man?" Kyle asked.

"He's fine." Mark dismissed him with a wave.

David regretted taking a hit as he thought of his team; he can't believe he had forgotten about them this entire time. He knew he wasn't allowed to do this, even if it was legal in his state, without a doctor's blessing. With the position he held inside the organization, they expected their workers to be of sound mind. It would leave his system before any drug test, though. David was sure of it.

His worried mind was quickly acquiesced as everything around him and inside of him seemed to move slower. The colors in the room began to brighten. His peripheral vision dampened and the world seemed to be shot in photos. Everything in his mind seemed to die down. David was apprehensive about all of this, but he really started to enjoy what he was feeling. He loved what this high provided for him. Maybe he could receive his doctor's blessing for this, since it so clearly helped him already.

He didn't even notice that Kyle started playing on the drums. Tim, at some point, joined him on the guitar. Mark rounded out the trio on the bass. They started to play and David didn't view it as just a wall of sound, he appreciated all of the individual notes on the guitar and bass as well as each beat of the drum.

David somehow found the rhythm of everything around him and pressed down on the keys to send out some transcendent synth. None of them were sure if this music was anything of worth, but it didn't stop the fun.

After finding some optimal sounds through the noise they were making, the practice was over.

David was finally coming down from his high so he thought it would be safe to drive back home now. Before he departed, Mark stopped him. "Here, take this."

It was marijuana and a bowl. David wasn't sure if he should accept; his gut told him no. "It's fine, man. Keep it."

"No, I insist." Mark responded with a wave in no particular direction.

David reluctantly took it. Maybe it would prove useful later.

He bid farewell to all three of them and made his way back home.

———————————

David arrived back home safely to find Joyce already fast asleep in their bed. He thought it was still early in the night, but he was wrong. Time flies when you're having fun.

He laid down on the bed next to her, on his left side, and held her as he tried to sleep.

Sleep did not come easy.

David felt a weird twitching beginning in his neck; it felt like his neck was being snapped by some specter. His head darted to the left side quickly, into his pillow, and just as quickly went back to its normal position. This happened about five times before he found his breath and the entire thing settled down for now.

He checked to see if he had awoken Joyce, but miraculously, she was still asleep. David thought for sure that was more chaotic and disruptive than it apparently was.

Even if it didn't wake Joyce, he still couldn't shake how scary that felt. What was wrong with him now? Was it the new medication? Was it the weed?

Whatever it was wasn't done with him. He felt it travel through his body. A strange ripple effect swept over him. It felt like something was trying to escape out of his body and leave his mortal coil behind.

David continued to seize and shake and his ultimate worry was, somehow, not waking his wife. His concern lay there and not on himself.

His neck continued to twitch rapidly and his body persisted with its shaking. David's body slowly eased, as if it exhausted itself, and he drifted into blissful sleep.

The bitter cold would not relent, but neither would he. The path kept going, to seemingly no end, but so did he.

He stopped; he saw something in the distance. A blackened core, he thinks, surrounded by blinding light. The core seemed to be an absence of anything and everything.

A figure loomed to the right of it. It had no discernable features from this distance. He kept walking towards the person and the core.

Towards the nothing. Towards the everything…

October 23rd, 2013

David tried to focus on setting up preliminary meetings with several free agents over the convulsing his body did last night as he tried to slumber. What was that last night? He would have to see what his doctor would say. Another appointment. He sighed to himself; they were becoming too frequent.

He was eyeing three names to strengthen his team: starting pitcher Zack Chronkite, outfielder Melvin Caba, and relief pitcher Kobi Zatura. David felt they would help deepen a beleaguered pitching staff and depleted outfield heading into the new campaign, which were the chief problems for his club last year.

David wandered from his desk to his bed. The TV spouted mindless nothing; he had forgotten it was even on. Probably something new and terrible happening in the world.

Joyce was fast asleep already, getting rested for her day of work tomorrow as well. David kissed her on the head, pulled the blanket up over him and tried to get some extra sleep.

David was hoping the interviews would go well tomorrow…

He saw a blinding light coming from the TV. He tried to move, but he couldn't. Total paralysis overtook him. He stared and stared, trying to escape this hypnotic light, while trying to make his way to it. To travel inside of this light.

Why? Was it time to die? He couldn't figure it out.

Let me out! He cried for help, yet no words came to fruition. All that came out was an awful, stifled scream, that was more of a moan of anguish…

David darted awake, panting and hyperventilating. What the hell was that? He thought. He was terrified and still unmoving under the covers; he was afraid to look around. David was fearful of what he might find staring back at him.

He finally worked up the courage to look at Joyce; she was still sound asleep. His cries did not wake her. How was she not awake? His cries were deafening, at least that's what David thought. It begged the question, were his pleas for help even real to begin with? Or were they contained inside of the dream world? David didn't know. All he knew was that he didn't want to go back to sleep and he didn't want to move, so he just lay there, helpless.

Did he imagine that? It felt so real. David felt paralyzed in his bed. What was wrong with him? It seemed like the dreams were starting to overtake him. Was it finally time to come clean with the doctor about it? He couldn't decide.

The panic and the fear finally subsided. The paralysis felt like it finally subsided so he got out of bed and went outside for some fresh air.

David needed something to calm his nerves. He remembered Mark's weed. That will bring me down, he thought to himself. He placed some in the bowl Mark had given him and he ripped it.

Almost instantly, he was brought back down. The terror and the dread that once existed inside of him was now gone. David loved this feeling; there was no worry and no stress. He felt so much better. The paralysis was a thing of the past within moments. The world slowed around him and put everything into perspective. David felt born anew after feeling completely helpless. The fog that was created by the dream world dissipated.

The combination of frenzied exhaustion and petrification by the nightmare and the marijuana helped him get to sleep once more. It was a whole new level of exhaustion for him.

It was a thing of the past, he told himself. Nothing to worry about.

October 24th, 2013

David set up the appointment on his own, without telling Joyce. He was too embarrassed about the sleep troubles and complications to talk to her about it; it made him feel like less of a man. He was even nervous to tell the doctor, for that matter. He thought about canceling the appointment numerous times earlier in the day, but he still came to the doctor's office, which was where he was at right now.

Here he sat, waiting to be called back. Should he fully come clean about the dreams? No, he didn't want to be deemed crazy. Should he leave right now and forget about it? Logically, he knew he shouldn't, but he wanted to. David really wanted to.

David sat there thinking about all of these doctor's visits he's had to go through already. Was it even worth it? Was there really some magic pill to help him feel better? Even when he did, there was always some side effect. One made him feel robotic. Another made him twitch and convulse in his sleep and, potentially, gave him the awful night terror he just recently had with the TV. Or were the night terrors just a morbid progression of the dreams he was already experiencing?

Either way, the other things were absolute net negatives as a result of the pills. Those side effects seemed to wash away all of the positives that the medications gave him. He became increasingly frustrated with it all.

"Room 19, David."

He nodded and made his way through the hallways to his room. He sat on the weird bed with the weird paper again, alone with his thoughts.

David had his preliminary meetings with the free agents he set up days prior, but he felt distracted. He hoped he didn't give off the wrong impression to his possible pickups.

What was taking the doctor so long?

The door opened and the nurse greeted him. She ran the normal scans and asked the routine questions, and then she left as David waited for the doctor once more.

It felt like he had lost control of his life completely. With the dreams, the deaths, the medications, and everything else, he didn't know what to do. It made him feel terrible about himself. David would do his damndest to get control over his mind and body once again.

"So, the medication isn't working out for you?" The doctor asked as she made her way into the room. "Again." She smiled.

"I…" he trailed off, wondering if any of this even actually happened to him or he made it up to feel alive, in some way. "I've been having…" He couldn't find the words.

"Take your time." The doctor reassured him.

"Thank you." David nodded to her. "So my neck is like snapping and twitching to one side and I'm not sure if it's the medication or what." David wanted to continue and talk about the dreams, but he ultimately kept that to himself once more. He remained terrified at the thought of what might happen.

"It seems like the medication is causing an overdose of serotonin and it's causing the body to seize up, in your case. That can cause different things, but that's what it's doing to you." The doctor was so sure of herself. David wished he felt that confident.

"I'll get you set up with another prescription," she continued, "and we'll wean you off of it the same way as we did the previous medication. Again, we all have different chemical makeups. We'll find the one that works." She left him with a smile and her classic wink as she departed.

David wished she shared her optimism. He couldn't help but feel pessimistic. Another medication and probably another failure. He felt like it was another ill-fated effort. What difference would it make? He wasn't sure how much more he could take.

Horror shook the frame of his new scene. A child, terrified at the thought of the presence of his father coming home. His mother was equally scared. He watched from the outside looking in. It was by him, for him.

What could he do to save himself? To save his mother? How could he get her out of this? He knew she wanted to leave him but froze at every possibility she had to do so.

The door opened and the story continued once more down the same road…

December 6th, 2013

The restaurant was dimly lit and seemingly a little higher class. Any light inside the establishment was a faint red. Joyce picked it out; she wanted a nice spot to have a somewhat nice goodbye dinner for David with Mark and Karen. David would be off to the Winter Summit once more next week.

David seemed to be happier with the third and, he hoped, final medication he was put on. He was feeling less pessimistic about life and was actually feeling excited about the dinner, but was still nervous, mainly about leaving for work. David was most excited to get more weed from Mark to keep his nerves calmed. He missed it. It's been David's biggest help in this battle across this past month. He was forced to take a bigger break than he wanted to, since he had to go back to work and pass his drug test, but he still wanted it for when he could finally smoke again.

He was excited to finally get some deals done. The Cosmos announced the signing of Zack Chronkite, the starting pitcher from the one meeting David had a month ago (he was hoping he could get Melvin Caba and Kobi Zatura as well, but they all remained unsigned; at least there was still time during the Winter Summit to reach an agreement). Chronkite was a good replacement for the knuckleballer Roger Alden, whom they announced the trade of around the same time, for a couple of minor leaguers. They also dumped the failure of Arik Knoll and his gaudy contract. The fans thought he was too late to trade Alden, claiming they were right for wanting to trade him a year ago when his value was highest, and shouldn't have signed Knoll to begin with, but David expected the vitriol. Damned if you do, damned if you don't.

"If you'll follow me…" The hostess interrupted his thoughts and took David and Joyce back to their reserved table. Mark and Karen were already seated. "Hey!" They exclaimed in unison.

"Drinking already?" David laughed as he pointed to the wine glasses at the table.

"They were provided to us unprompted." Mark shrugged.

Both couples embraced each other one-by-one. Joyce felt like her hug with Mark lasted a bit too long. The feeling of the hug sparked something in her memory again, like the handshake at the party. Something deep from her past called to her. Something so far away and so close. Something old, something new.

"It's nice to finally sit down and have dinner like this. How long has it been since we've done anything like this together?" Joyce said.

"Too long, honey." Karen said. "We've been looking forward to this as well for quite some time."

"David says you run a clothing company?" Mark cut into the small talk. Him and Joyce really didn't get to know each other that well at his birthday party.

"Yes, it's going quite well. Been a long time coming, but we just hit our stride and took off over the past couple of years. Finally got a store and everything." Joyce smiled.

"Well, congrats!" Mark said. They clinked their mimosa-filled glasses, the ones that were provided at the outset of the meal.

Joyce continued, "I realized we never talked about work at the party."

"Well, it was a party." Karen said; they all laughed.

"Fair enough." Joyce continued, "So what do you two do?"

"I've worked out of this music store since I was 16." Karen replied. "We also do movies and games and all the media stuff, really. It's not glamorous but I've always enjoyed it. The perks are nice after climbing the ladder as well."

"I feel stupid. You definitely told me that already at the party." Joyce facepalmed herself, clearly embarrassed at how stupid she felt. "My apologies."

"Don't worry, I love to brag when I can." Karen added jokingly. "Like how we get these great paid vacations to various destinations. You gotta put in the work, of course, to get the best regional manager awards and all that, but they pay handsomely."

"I'm actually unemployed currently." Mark avoided eye contact as he butted into the conversation again. Why did he make it about himself again? David thought. It seemed like Karen had more to say there.

"Really? What happened?" Joyce paused. "If you don't mind me asking."

"After you've done the same thing over and over, it just gets kind of old. I wanted out so I just used my situation to my advantage, honestly."

"Which means…?"

"It was snowy one evening. I probably could have made it in, if I really wanted to, but I decided to call off. I knew I was over on points, but I got fired because of it. Since it was really bad and inclement weather, unemployment accepted me. The warehouse work was wearing on me. I just wanted, no, I needed an out. I'll get back on my feet soon."

"I know you will." Karen rubbed his arm lovingly.

"That makes a lot of sense." David agreed. "Warehouse work is rough. I used to do it before I got my job within the Cosmos organization." When David said that, something in Joyce's memory sparked again. But why?

"Yeah, I'm just looking for something new now." Mark turned back to Joyce and looked at her while he continued; it was like he only wanted her as an audience. "Something completely different. I want to feel like my job carries some weight, like it matters to someone. Not just some number for some soulless corporation." He paused. "I'm thinking about doing something in the mental health field."

"That would be awesome!" Joyce exclaimed. "David wanted to do that when we were younger and dating." Her memory sparked again at that comment. Mark just reminded her of David. That was it. They were like the same person; she could see why they got along so well.

"I fell off pretty hard." David joked and put his hands up as if he was busted for some crime.

"Nah," Mark piped up, either missing the joke or steamrolling over it to make a point, "you're still helping people with baseball and giving people entertainment. An escape."

"The fans certainly don't think so."

"Ah, it was only one year." Mark dismissed it with a wave. "You excited to leave for the team?" Mark had a devilish grin on his face.

"I am." David said. "I'm very nervous, though. I just want to do a good job. I want the fans to see a winner again. They deserve it."

"Don't worry too much. Your hard work will pay off. I just know it." Joyce rubbed his arm lovingly.

David turned to Joyce in the passenger seat as they drove home from the restaurant. "What did you think?"

"I thought the restaurant was nice and it was fun to catch up with them after what? A month?"

"Yeah, I'm glad I met them. I'm glad you like them, too."

"I'm glad you met them as well. Your mood seems like it has vastly improved since you did."

"Really?"

"Oh, definitely."

"Well, that's good. I can't say I've taken notice too much."

"Why's that?"

"I feel like it's… it's still there. Just kind of waiting. Waiting to be activated again… or something. And the first two medications sure haven't inspired much hope." David felt himself shut down. So much to say with no place to start.

"It's a process." Joyce consoled. "It'll take time to heal. Trauma like this isn't easy to get through. It doesn't magically solve itself overnight. Just take the small victories, like your improved mood. And the fact that this medication hasn't had any side effects so far." She held his right hand on the center console. David still seemed distant to her.

Joyce tried to help out as much as she could, but it still didn't feel like enough. All she could do was hold him and be there for him as a shoulder to cry on. All she could do was simply be there.

It was becoming somewhat exhausting, if she was honest with herself. It seemed like nothing helped and it was draining on her in her everyday life. That made her feel awful, since David was clearly going through a tumultuous time. But so was she.

Joyce thought that maybe talking about nothing would help. "What helps me is holding onto my stuffed animals." David gave a weak smile in return; he knew she was trying. It felt like after the nice high of being with his friends, he was coming down hard. Why was his depression poking back through the veil of his medication now?

His mind fluttered back to what Joyce was saying. David always did love small things about Joyce, like her stuffed animals; it was so innocent and cute to him. Maybe her aimless talk was helping a little bit.

"It just helps release all of the feelings, I guess." She continued, "I also like to clean, to keep my mind occupied, even for a little bit." David still sat, like a stone. He wasn't sure what to say. He wasn't sure what to offer. His previous feelings seemed to be coming back up once more. Feelings he thought he had long since left behind.

"I know you haven't put up any pictures of them or anything," Joyce felt uncomfortable with the silence, so she kept talking, "but that might help. It reminds us that they are still alive and well, in our memories. Looking out for us and watching over us." She paused momentarily. "Even when we poop." That got a laugh out of David, but still no words. Joyce was content with a laugh.

David was happy she was trying to help, but it really didn't offer much. Words, thoughts and prayers, all of it seemed so hollow to him. So unhelpful. Was there anything to help him?

After arriving back home, she quickly grabbed his arm as they walked to the house, linked like a chain. David appreciated the closeness and the help, even if he couldn't express it.

They laid on the couch and bundled up to cuddle. Their cuddling sparked something in David that he hadn't felt in a while: a strong urge to show love physically. How long had it been? They've been so preoccupied with life and death that it felt like an eternity since they had done it. They both craved it more than they knew.

Foreplay quickly commenced which brought them just as quickly to their bedroom. They hadn't done this for a while and Joyce was exploding at the thought, now thrilled it was a reality; she didn't know how much she missed it until it came back around.

David was aroused, but, shamefully, he couldn't finish. After the fact, he laid there, sad and embarrassed, with Joyce stroking his hair as he rested his head in her bosom.

The shaking fired back up; he was pulsating, the advent of the twitching and convulsing at his heels and quickly rising through his frame. The feeling of something inside of him, trying to escape his body. His soul felt like it was transcending from his carnal frame; his soul felt like it was trying to live outside of him and leave him behind. His head was seizing and twitching, back and forth, back and forth into her chest. A swirl of emotions. Anger, hate, sadness, shame, because of everything he was as a human being. Another failure. Another futile effort. Was this all he'll ever be? A shell of himself?

Joyce was there next to him, holding him. Being held by her helped him minimally, but his physical and mental deficiencies remained. She cared for and loved him but David felt she did not deserve this wretch of a man he had become. She should have something better. She deserved a normal man and a normal life. David kept shaking and twitching, wanting to leave but locked in place…

The wood creaks under his feet. The plank bent with his weight on it. He was being forced to sea by people he thought were his brethren.

What did he do to deserve this? Wrongly accused, wrongly sent to his death. How could he prove it to them?

It was too late. One more step and he was lost to the ocean blue. Down, down, down to the abyssal plain.

He plunged deep into the water; it was cold and hopeless. The weight around his neck pulled him farther down to the depths of the sea floor. He gasped for water and tried to swim, but it did nothing. The weight around his neck was too much.

He gave up. He resigned to his fate. A death for him and him alone…

December 7th, 2013

Suddenly, David darted awake. He didn't even remember falling asleep. All David remembered was the terrible seizing and the shame of what he couldn't do.

David looked at Joyce and she was fast asleep. How much more could she take? David felt horrible for putting her through this. He flipped over in their bed to the clock to his right and it was very early in the morning. It was so early that he still considered it night and the sky agreed with him.

He recollected his dreams; they have become so vivid and downright frightening. They seemed so real, yet so far beyond him. He felt a loss of a grip on his own reality while trying to grasp one so far away.

David felt a calling to this part of him. How could he meet this portion of himself? Was that portion even himself? He would have to be ready for the dreams. He would have to be ready to fight back. He would have to be ready to take them over…

There she lay on the bed; a collection of tubes and wires. She was about to pass on into the next world.

He regretted not seeing her in her final hours. How could he be so selfish? She was what was important and he made it about himself. Selfish.

The only constant in his life was about to fade into memory. The foundation of his life was about to crumble and break apart. No more guiding light. He would have to find his way on his own…

David woke up that morning after another haunting dream and laid there motionless. He was petrified still and, after a minute of not knowing what to do, his body went into another seizing episode. This woke Joyce up; she held him tight from behind.

"Hey, hey," she lovingly stated, "it's okay." She brushed his hair with her hand. "Do you think it's the medication they just put you on?"

David did not respond.

Joyce continued, "I think you need to go back to the doctor. If this medication is causing all of this."

"So they can just put me on something else that won't work?" David raised his voice fractionally to Joyce; he felt bad about that instantly. He was clearly annoyed, but he felt justified about it. All these pills and they all caused pain instead of healing. At the end of the day, it wasn't Joyce's fault.

Joyce remained calm. She either didn't notice him raising his voice, which seemed unlikely, or chose to remain as diplomatic as possible. "It's frustrating, but there is something that is going to work."

"I really doubt that." David believed that wholeheartedly. He also, plain and simple, did not feel like going to the doctor again either. He just wanted to lay there all day. Joyce felt this residing in him.

"I'll schedule you an appointment." She paused. "I hate to leave you like this, but I have to go to the mall and check on the store." Joyce said. With that, she kissed his cheek and started off to the mall, leaving David all alone, by himself.

After about an hour and half of being virtually lifeless, David decided to get out of bed. Should he shower? He decided against it. David didn't want to.

He flipped on the TV and it was already on the PBL Network.

"...it's two months into the off-season and while some teams have been active, there have been others not so much. Including the Cold Creek Cosmos."

"They've made some moves." The co-anchor played devil's advocate.

"Not enough for a team that, just this past season, was under .500!" The first analyst continued,

"A lot of pain has surrounded that club this past year and they need more than what David Renninger has done. Aside from his press conference, the General Manager has seemingly ghosted his own team." The analyst laughed at his own wit. He paused and amended somewhat. "The pain is not without its reasoning. David Renninger suffered some grave losses in his personal life throughout the year."

"Yeah," the other reporter picked up the thread, "it was a rough inaugural year for him. There is still a lot of time left in this offseason. Plus The Winter Summit doesn't officially begin for another couple of days anyways. Although, a lot of fans are giving him zero sympathy. They still want him out of the job after a failed year and now this excruciating inactivity."

He cut the TV off and put on a streaming service. His anger rose and, after all that he had been through already, it led to welling tears. David needed to calm down, so he got up and grabbed the bag of weed that Mark gave him. Should he even do this with The Winter Summit coming right around the corner? David's thoughts were cut off as he checked his vibrating phone.

It was Mark.

The text read: "Wanna jam later?"

David saw it and didn't feel like responding. Didn't we have a goodbye dinner for a reason? He wanted Mark to go away. He was too exhausted. He just flat out didn't want to do anything, but he also did not want to let him down. David felt bad for his displaced feelings of anger towards him and Joyce. The war raged.

David decided on not opening it and left it to linger for a future time. Right now, he just wanted to smoke.

He was falling into a fresh void, but he numbed the pain and fed the end as he wasted away on his couch, bit by bit. The only thing he wanted to do was watch pointless squabbles inside of an office.

Hours were quickly being lost, but he felt like he was wearing the eyes of millenia with how much time slowed for him…

Joyce left the store after doing her rounds and checking in with everyone and everything. She peered up from her purse and looked and thought she recognized a face. She squinted and, yes, it was Mark. What a coincidence! She thought.

"Mark?!" Joyce exclaimed.

"Joyce?" Mark questioned back before they hugged. "Fancy seeing you here, huh?"

"Yeah, what brings you here?"

"Just some mindless window shopping." Mark motioned to the video game store he was standing next to. "Celebrating getting my new job a bit. You?"

"Checking on the store. About to head back. That's great to hear you finally got a job! Was it the job helping out with mental illness that you talked about the other night?"

"Correct. It felt like I was never gonna get an interview, with how long ago I had applied, but I'm glad I finally got one." Mark paused for dramatic effect. "And I nailed it." He pumped his fist.

"That's awesome! Congratulations!"

"Thank you." Mark quickly changed the subject. "Have you heard from David? I tried to get a hold of him and he hasn't answered. Gotta make a decision on my night here shortly."

"Nothing on my end. Kind of a rough go of it for him." Joyce quickly backtracked because she didn't want to get into it or talk behind David's back about him. "He's probably packing and getting ready for his trip."

"Really? What's going on?"

"Not sure I want to get into it, honestly." Joyce knew she had said too much.

"Please, I insist." Mark pointed to a bench and beckoned her to come. She reluctantly gave in and joined.

"So… what's up?" Mark asked.

"Well… just a rough go of it with his latest medication." Joyce responded.

"How so?"

Joyce gritted her teeth and let out a sound. She didn't want to get into it. Mark picked up on that, but persisted.

"I used to be on medication myself for that type of thing." Joyce wished he would just stop talking. "More anxiety than anything, but I went through a lot of them. With a lot of nasty side effects." There it was again. Something Joyce couldn't shake. Something old, something new.

"Honestly," he continued, "still the worst for me to this day was… not being able to perform…" he gesticulated wildly, "you know."

"That's what…" She trailed off, not thinking before she said it, but knew she said too much. With a look of realization, Mark knew what was wrong now.

"I've said too much. I'll see ya later." Joyce was in mid stride to get up, but Mark grabbed her forearm and gave her a reassuring glance. A ripple was sent through her once more. She fell back down on the bench.

"It's okay, I understand. It really does suck." He rubbed her forearm with his thumb. Something old, something new. "Since he probably doesn't want to talk, send him my best wishes." He hugged her again as they sat on the bench, and it was much more uncomfortable than the last.

Joyce was left to wonder again why he was so familiar.

December 8th, 2013

David left the doctor's office with a brand new medication that he had no interest in taking. It was some more of the same; a rhetoric about different chemical makeups, how they'll find the right one, blah blah, blah. The first made him feel robotic, the second made him seize before he slept, and the third made him not be able to perform sexually. Now, he faces an unknown in this fourth medication, which he had no intention of finding out.

After ghosting him for a day, David finally got back to Mark, saying he was concerned about his appointment and didn't want to talk the day prior; he would go over there to jam tonight. Mark kept pestering him about it, for whatever reason, since the dinner. David was torn; he wanted to go but didn't want to all the same. There was no backing out now, though. David was on his way to pick Mark up now.

"Thanks for coming to grab me." Mark got into his passenger seat, looking beyond disheveled.

"You look like you've walked for miles."

"Thanks for the compliment." Mark smirked. "How did the appointment go?"

"It happened." David replied. "I got another new medication so that's… good."

"Oh yeah, Joyce was telling me about the other medication not working the other day."

How much did she say? David wondered. He got angry at the thought. "Uhh... yeah."

"Did I tell you I finally got a job?"

"Oh, no, you didn't. That's great to hear." David couldn't care less about whatever job he got. It made him feel bad, but the numbness was becoming too great.

"Yeah, I'll be helping out people with mental illnesses, like I said at the dinner. I'm excited to finally do something worthwhile."

David nodded his head and feigned happiness and a smile. He was happy for him but there were more pressing things on his mind than this, so it smothered his joy for a friend.

"Hey, can you stop at a gas station? I need to get some energy." Mark asked. David nodded his head and obliged as he pulled into the parking lot.

The bell rang as they entered and the clerk beamed with joy at the sight of Mark, like he was a long lost friend. "You're here later than normal." Clearly, Mark frequented this particular gas station quite a bit.

"Yeah, we're going to practice and I'm already yawning." Mark joked.

"Just the coffee then, Max?"

"It's Mark. Did you just have a stroke?" Mark laughed and turned to David. "Did you need anything?"

"No, I'm good." David replied. The look on the attendant's face was strange to David. It didn't seem like he made a mistake there.

They left the gas station and rode on in silence. As they approached the house, the sight of flashing lights, red and blue and white, took center stage. Ambulances and police vehicles were in the driveway of Kyle's home.

They had to park on the street and walk to the garage. "What the hell?" Mark raced out ahead of David.

'Do Not Enter' tape surrounded the house. "We need you to move along." The cop commanded as they came upon the garage.

"This is my friend's home." Mark was rapidly becoming heated with the officer. There was clearly some innate disdain towards authority. "I know them. We were coming here for band practice. How many more reasons do you need?" The cop did not give in. "What's going on, dammit? I have a right to know."

The cop didn't answer but David and Mark caught the glimpse of the garage around the rotund figure of the officer. Kyle and Tim were both laid out on the floor lifeless. David couldn't tell anything besides that, but he knew they were long gone.

David came home, stunned and shocked. He wished he had felt more, to know that he was still human, but he just felt even more numb. Joyce was waiting on the couch. She knew something was off.

"Is everything okay?" She asked.

"No. Kyle and Tim were found dead today. Not really sure what happened." He sighed and shook his head. "This world is madness." He laughed hollowly.

"That's horrible." She lept off of the couch and wrapped her arms around him. "Do you think they were murdered?"

"They didn't say, but they seemed to rule that out. Accidental overdose seems to be the prevailing cause." He remembered seeing the syringes on the ground next to him. It reminded him of Sam. David shook his head as he sat down on the couch; Joyce joined him.

"I got a new medication today, though." David continued with no proper segue. He wanted to change the subject since he wasn't sure how he felt about two people he didn't know all that well passing away.

"Did you start taking it?"

"Not yet, I will tomorrow." He paused, remembering something from earlier today. "What did you say to Mark?"

Joyce didn't expect that but didn't want to seem defensive. She really didn't do anything wrong; Joyce had the info coerced out of her.

"I told him that you were having a rough go of it with the medication."

"And nothing else?"

"No… but-"

"Did you tell him what happened?" He glowered deeply at her. "What exactly happened because of the medication?"

Joyce got defensive, against her better judgment. "He got it out of me, I swear." Her voice was higher than she intended it to be. "Mark said it had happened to him before as well."

The anger inside of David had been bubbling for a while. For many months, for a year, and now he couldn't contain it anymore.

"How dare you fucking tell him that? That's a private problem. An embarrassing problem. You had no fucking right!" David stood up; a commanding presence over Joyce on the couch.

"I swear, it just slipped." Joyce's voice was a helpless shout.

This enraged him even further. How dare she talk right now? How dare she even try to defend this?

David lashed out; he didn't strike Joyce, but he struck everything else in the room. The TV, the game systems, the computer, the desks, the coffee table; it all met his wrath. He grabbed the door handle and flung the door against the wall, creating a hole in it with the doorknob.

"Please don't go!" Joyce cried out to David.

David did not or chose not to hear it, as he stormed out into the night. Where he was going he wasn't sure of.

Joyce floated to the door frame. "Please don't go." She whispered into the endless night.

———

Joyce was left devastated and numb. She opened her phone, trying to distract herself and saw a message from Mark: "How's David doing? I'm worried about him after what we saw tonight."

She replied: "He didn't even seem fazed by that. He's just angry that I told you about what happened."

"Do you need anything? I can come over."

"No, it's okay."

"Seriously, I want to help."

She relented and said it was okay for him to come over. It was all so much for Joyce to process. This whole year felt like it finally reached its culmination. What was left for Joyce to do? It felt like she couldn't save David and she was tired of trying. Where did that leave her?

Mark knocked on the door and she opened it to let him in. "What the hell happened?" He looked around the room; it looked like a tornado dropped down only on the Renninger household. "Are you okay?"

"No." Joyce laughed. How could she be okay? She knew it was just a general question, though, and that he was trying to help. "I just wish he would understand. I didn't mean to say anything." She went back to sit down on the couch.

Mark followed her like a puppy to the couch. "Yeah, this was my fault. I can't believe he took it out on you." Mark grabbed her hand. She pulled it from his grasp.

"No, I-"

"I'm sorry, that's not what I intended. Just trying to comfort you."

"No, I'm sorry." She looked away from Mark. "I-I'm overreacting. I just-I don't know." She gave him a hug. Joyce felt a rush of emotions. Relief. Longing. Sadness. Guilt. Familiarity.

The hug ended and she looked into his ocean blue eyes. She knew those eyes. She remembered those eyes. Something old. Something new.

"I think you should leave." Joyce abruptly got up from the couch, raced to the door, and opened it for Mark.

Mark walked up to the door and stopped to face her again. "If you need anything, I'm here." He clasped her arm and he left.

Joyce closed the door behind him and felt every emotion humanly possible.

She really wanted him to stay.

December 9th, 2013

David finally left for the Winter Summit. Depending on the viewpoint, the timing of it all was the worst or the best.

The argument with Joyce was the biggest in their entire relationship. Part of him felt bad for what he did, but he felt justified with how he reacted. Trust was fractured and privacy was out of the window.

After he stormed out, David came back in the morning to grab his things. They barely said anything to each other as he left. They feigned care and love and gave each other a kiss, which felt automatic, like they were just supposed to. They still did love each other, but they felt cold to each other.

On top of that, David was on his new medication and it was only making things worse, in a new and horrendous way.

He barely wanted to get up today for his flight (now, whether that was because of the meds or the fight was anybody's guess) and he barely wanted to stay either; he wanted to be somewhere in the middle. David could feel the darkness slowly creeping back in, with everything happening in his life currently and the blackness that has shadowed his life perpetually this year. It felt like they became one and it has begun to slowly eat him alive again. The medication seemed to be compounding everything and plunging him even further down.

Was this all his fault? He was the one that didn't perform. It wasn't Joyce's fault it slipped out. Or was it? David's lack of performance was the reason that it was even a thought to begin with. It was all on him.

Shut up, David told his mind. He had to refocus. It was time to get to work. He would have to get some sleep on the plane.

He ran down the hall. Tears streamed down his face. His heart was filled with sadness. He just stared down the eyes of a withering coil previously known as a man.

He couldn't believe how little time he had left and how little he wanted to spend any of it with him. He didn't want to see him that way, he couldn't, so he ran and ran, by himself...

Joyce hadn't told David about what almost happened.

Would she have kissed Mark last night? She certainly wanted to, but she stopped herself.

Why did she even want to? Was it everything that was going wrong within her relationship? Or was she legitimately developing feelings for this man? She felt the guilt of not being honest with David, but after all that had happened between them, did it matter that much?

Why was Mark so familiar? She couldn't shake the feeling that she felt. His eyes were something she had seen before and almost overtook her completely.

Joyce just needed to distance herself from this man. It was the longing of something she hadn't felt for awhile with David. That was all it was. It was only natural.

Mark started his new job today. The job was basically at a house; the homliness was intended to help comfort the patients at the facility with the mental problems. At least, that's what he was told by his boss.

The ill people needed around the clock care and vigilance, and that's what Mark helped with. Most of the residents were suffering from deeply suicidal thoughts and needed help being talked down. Mark and his coworkers were there to help keep them afloat.

The others dealt with that and drug addiction, which only compounded the aforementioned mental problems. A drug epidemic still surged through his home area. It made Mark feel a range of emotions.

He had a lot on his mind as well. The death of Kyle and Tim and what happened with Joyce and David. What almost happened afterwards as well.

Mark tried to think positively with both incidents.

Mark was very appreciative of the time he had spent with his two friends but he sincerely missed jamming with them. It was discovered that they both accidentally overdosed; he knew they had problems with harder drugs, but he could only do so much. It was all a part of the plan decided long ago. That same plan brought him here and now to continue onward with his mission for his home area and the world.

And then last night. He could see it in Joyce's eyes. She wanted him and he'd be lying if he said he didn't reciprocate those feelings. What could he do with that? Nothing now and probably nothing later. Wherever the plan willed him, he would go, he supposed. He just took it as a compliment that someone felt that way about him. There was nothing else he could do since he was with Karen.

He just didn't want things to be awkward with Joyce, or, for that matter, David, from here on out. They were both still dear friends to him. It saddened him that neither of them sent him messages of good luck for his first day on the job. What could he do? They were both quite busy, he guessed.

Mark didn't want to dwell, he had to be laser-focused, especially with this job. He didn't want to feel anything that had happened over the past 24 hours. It would slow him down on his mission for this world, which would continue at this job.

December 31st, 2013

It was New Year's Eve and a lot had changed. Everything felt different.

David and Joyce were surrounded by a brand new couple in Mark and Karen, instead of Sam and Liz. Neither David or Joyce felt the same about them being there over Sam and Liz, for different reasons.

There was a tension in the air. A month had passed since their big argument and nothing had improved since. David and Joyce's engagement was on hold for now; they canceled their date to be wed on January 11th when they were apart for The Winter Summit. He knew there was something lingering that

Joyce wasn't telling him about. Was there unfinished business from the argument? Or was it something entirely different?

It was a far cry from the bliss they felt last New Year's Eve.

David felt like he was drifting farther and farther away from the world, and his failing relationship didn't help. Was he losing his mind? He should have come clean about the dreams and sought help. It was affecting everything. How much more could he run?

"The wind is pretty strong tonight." Karen broke the ice, literally and figuratively; there was a coating of ice on the sidewalk that crunched as she said it. The winter came back stronger than ever but, to be frank, it felt like it never really left. All four of them were standing outside in the bitter cold; Mark and David smoked. He continued to smother the void…

They all nodded in agreement with Karen. Mark turned to David. "How did the Winter Summit go?"

"Fine." He coughed through inhalation. "We got the other two guys I wanted earlier, and a couple of others, and I'm very happy about it. I'm definitely gonna prove people wrong next year." David smiled, but he felt no joy.

David felt his phone vibrate. "I have to take this." He rushed inside.

"That's a good idea. It's too cold." Karen nodded towards David. "I'm gonna head inside as well." She turned to Mark, "You coming?"

"I'll stay outside for a minute. The cold will perk me up." Mark smiled.

"Okay. See you inside… whenever." She shrugged with a giggle and went inside.

Joyce turned to follow Karen, but Mark grabbed her arm as Karen disappeared through the entryway. "Wait."

"I don't-"

"Please." Mark eyes told the entire story. They called to Joyce again. "We have to talk about this."

"There's nothing to talk about." She just wanted to leave, but she felt rooted in place. She wanted to say so much. She wanted to do so much. "Look, I-"

She was cut off as Mark leaned in and kissed her. Joyce tried to reject it, she tried to relent, but she couldn't help it. Something old. Something new. It felt magical, like a long lost lover returned to her.

"You failed the drug test." The team president said. "I told you, one more slip up and we would have to let you go." Gaylord sighed deeply. "I had so much faith in you." The disappointment was strong in his voice.

"No, please-" The call cut out; the president hung up on David. The anger and sadness came up again all at once, intertwined. How far could he fall? This was all his fault.

He opened the door to go tell Joyce and realized that he could, indeed, fall further.

"What are you doing?" David was shouting. He wasn't sure how loud he was.

"It's not what you think." Mark pulled himself from Joyce and tried to plead with David. All David saw was red.

David rushed towards Mark; Joyce slid out of the way and landed softly on the icy concrete. David clocked Mark with a right hook. He fell backwards over the rock, before sliding off to the ground below; Mark's back howled over the cold stone.

"David, stop!" Joyce cried out to him.

David could barely hear her. There was only one thing on his mind: violence. How could Mark do this to him? He brought the drugs to him, costing him his job. Now, he was infiltrating his relationship.

He straddled his chest to keep Mark still and he continued to rain down lefts and rights. Mark held up his arms in a defensive position to lessen the blows. "You son of a bitch! Why?" Anger was boiling inside of him. Tears were streaming down his face. David didn't even care that the shots weren't true or connecting with anything vital.

"What is going on?" Karen raced to the door frame, hearing the commotion. The horror dawned quickly on her. "Get off of him, you monster!"

Karen tried to pull David off of Mark, but to no avail. "Why are you doing this?"

"He ruined my life. He ruined everything!" The fists continued to pour down before he finally exhausted himself. Mark's forearms were essentially one full bruise.

David was hyperventilating as he stood up from his assault. Karen started to pound his chest with fists of her own, but they barely registered.

Karen picked up Mark and rested him on the lawn chair. His face was slightly bloodied from the inaugural punch and it looked like a tooth was missing as well. "Why did you do this?"

"He cost me my job. Fed me his fucking drugs and got me fired." David's voice was monotone and foreboding.

"He didn't do that," Karen was hysterical, "you did that. You had a choice."

Joyce could not contain her emotions; she weeped on the outside of the scene. David looked at Joyce; the audacity to weep right now, he thought. The exhaustion consumed him fully and he sat down on the rock Mark collided with. "He kissed Joyce." It was almost a whisper.

"What?" Karen somehow heard it.

David looked at her. "You heard me." David's breathing was heavy and shallow. "He kissed Joyce."

Karen had a flash of emotions register over her face. She turned to Mark, then to Joyce. Back to Mark. Back to Joyce.

"Do you have nothing to say?" David turned to Joyce.

She continued to cry and mouthed the words 'I'm sorry' that almost came out in a whisper.

David got over his anger about her crying; he realized why she was crying in the first place. "This is all my fault." David was now thinking out loud. "I caused all of this." David stood up from the rock and departed for the door.

"Please." Joyce was basically whispering; she couldn't find her voice.

"Wait for me." Karen followed closely behind David, but he barely registered that.

He sat in the car and just waited. He almost thought Joyce would race after him. Why wasn't she? She didn't love him anymore, that's why. It was all his fault.

David was stunned, unmoving. He was lost in his own world. Disconnected from reality.

Karen thumped on the passenger side window and broke David from his thoughts. "Open the door." She said, "I'm coming with you."

David grunted in response and unlocked the door. He pulled out of the driveway and they left.

"I feel so selfish and so stupid. Why did you do that? You should leave!" Joyce was pacing, not as quickly as her thoughts were racing, while Mark was on the couch. The TV hummed softly in the background. They were left in the aftermath. The wake. She collected her breath. "No, you shouldn't go anywhere. It's not your fault. Are you okay?"

Mark held the ice to his face. "No." He laughed. "Thanks for taking care of me, though." He motioned to the ice pack.

"Of course." Joyce paused. "I can't believe he did that. He's never been violent before."

"He's been through a lot this year."

"That still doesn't make it okay."

Mark shrugged his shoulders.

"I just feel like he doesn't get it and he hasn't all year." Joyce continued, "I've been through a lot, too. I lost the same friends and I held up as best as I could." She shook her head. "What am I saying? Comparing emotions. Trying to justify my own shortcomings."

"Your emotions aren't shortcomings."

"How are they not?" She joined Mark on the couch. "They've caused all of this distress. I cheated on him. He didn't deserve this."

"No, you didn't deserve this." Mark brought the ice down and looked into her eyes. "He caused you so much grief. He didn't take his problems seriously and made you worry all the time."

"Stop."

"He started the rift in your relationship. He just wanted to use you. He guilted you into staying with him, even though you deserved better."

"I said stop."

"It had nothing to do with the medication. It had nothing to do with random urges. You were deprived all year, because he was being sad and mopey and using you for secondary gain. He can make this world what he wants and he chose to have you suffer."

"Stop!" Joyce slapped Mark hard across the face, right where David punched him. "I'm so sorry." She grabbed his hand and brought the ice up to his face again.

"It's fine." Mark winced. "I probably deserved that."

"No, you didn't." Joyce placed her hand across his chin and rubbed gently.

The TV interjected, without emotion.

"...10, 9..."

Her hand fell to the nape of his neck and she pulled him close.

"...6, 5..."

Mark brought the ice down from his face and leaned in.

'...2, 1....:"

She kissed him fully on the lips.

Joyce wanted even more as the clock struck midnight.

"Can you believe him?" It was the first and only thing David heard of Karen's ranting. He nodded when it felt needed before that. How long had they been driving?

David was knee deep into his own mind. It was empty, it was nothing, and it was everything.

Did he even care? Was this the punctuation mark on something already written? Maybe the bottom of the bottle would know.

Joyce is the girl of his dreams. Or should he say was? Was there any repair for what just happened? Of what has happened over the past year? David was barely himself anymore. He was barely a person.

David wanted to blame himself for this. He was angry. What could he have done to prevent this? He could have done something. Right?

The latest medication forced his mind to turn on him; it seemed to ramp up his dark thoughts. David rolled down the window, grabbed the drugs out of the center console, and hucked the pill bottle out of the car on their way to the bar. It sent him further into the black over the past month and throwing them out of the window seemed to be the only logical way to cast it all away. With what just transpired, his life was even worse. Would this finally be the last straw?

David had yet to find the exact reason to blame himself for all of this. Yet. He knew it was on its way.

They were departing from the bar. When did they get to the bar? He turned and saw Karen walking next to him. She was still here? David couldn't believe it. He could barely believe he was still alive. He was beyond plastered; Karen should probably drive. Who's Karen again? Oh well, he drove anyway.

Karen continued to blabber next to him, David was transfixed by a light pole he saw up ahead. What would happen if he flipped the car into metal and wrapped himself around it? He thought. It flickered and passed. The light pole faded from his sight as he continued to drive.

Karen was now out cold in the passenger seat; apparently she wasn't fit to drive either. David remembered her saying she would try to work this out with Mark somehow.

Another light pole up ahead. The same thought. What would happen if he flipped into it?

So he did.

Suspended in the black again, he can't swim. What else was new?

It's nothing. It's everything. It's all he is and all he wasn't. It's all he will become…

January 11th, 2014

"…have parted ways with David Renninger." The TV blurted out. It gave way to the president of the Cold Creek Cosmos. "'It's been a long and stressful year for David. We hope he can finally get better, we hope he can seek help, but as an organization, we've done all we could. As a business and out of respect to our fans, we all need to move on. This was a mutual decision. We want to win…'"

It had been almost two weeks since the accident; Karen was in a coma and David was in rehab for his drug and alcohol addiction. He had also come clean about the dreams during his initial hospital visit; they would send him to a mental institution after he got clean of his drug addiction. The clear mind would help him get everything sorted out. Or so they said.

Mark was thinking of pressing charges against David for the accident and damage done, alongside the physical assault David handed him, but he decided against it.

Joyce was allowed to visit David that day. It would all be out in the open.

This was it.

"How are things going in here?" Joyce asked.

"Fine." David couldn't say anything more. A lingering, tense silence intensified between them.

Moments that felt like eternity passed. "Look, this has been an awful year for you and I get that. I do. But I've been going through it as well." Joyce paused, making sure she would say exactly the right words. "I understand that you were working and fighting your own battles and I was there for you, through all of it. Even when you didn't want me to be and even now, I'm here for you because you were dismissed as general manager. All of this left me alone."

She was trying to hold back tears. She still felt selfish about this, but it needed to be said. "I want to preface this by saying, nothing more has come from this, but I slept with Mark on New Year's. I needed something. You left me alone and left me to face all of this alone. I lost friends, too, and I had no comfort until he came along." Joyce paused and looked deep into David's eyes. "Did you know we were supposed to be married today? We made a vow to be wed on Liz's birthday. It was supposed to be a happy day; a beginning and a remembrance. Now, it's nothing. I've been here for over a half an hour, not that I think you even understand that, and you haven't mentioned anything about either of those things since I've been here with you today. You haven't helped me at all today. All I've thought of today is the loss of our wedding and the loss of her. She was my closest friend, like Sam to you.

"I'm a rambling mess," she continued, "but I'm sorry that I did what I did. I should have been more open than I was. Maybe we could have avoided all of this if I was." Joyce looked at David. "That's all I have to say."

David stared into the floor the entire time. He finally found the reason. It was his fault.

"I'm sorry I did this to you." David smiled a weak smile and then he left back to his room.

That was it.

Mark pulled the razor from the client. She was trying to end it all in the bathroom at his job. She didn't see much of a reason to live anymore. She had seen the world fall apart around her. The mad world was closing in on another.

This was one of his toughest clients, but Mark finally got a hold of her. He had a firm grasp of her wrist and finally pulled the razor from her hand. "You aren't leaving yet." He said sternly.

She dove for him and knocked him down on the ground; the blade fell to the bathroom floor. He could feel his head jar and the bruises and scars from his fight with David twinged with pain. The patient scurried towards the razor, but reinforcements came. Two fellow coworkers grabbed her arms and carried her away. She would be under close surveillance for the rest of the night after this recent outburst. Mark grabbed the razor blade as he left the room.

Mark dismissed the two helpers and came into her room, trying to talk her down. He embraced her, even if it was against protocol, and held her tight. He tried to develop trust, but would it actually work? Even if it did, how much good would it do for her?

This lady was Mark's first personal client and he's done the best job he could to keep her tethered to the earth. Mark was starting to lose hope; it seemed like it was only a matter of time until she was gone. It was like she was gone already, so what did it matter?

He left her behind for another day. Until tomorrow with her again. Or maybe not.

Overall, the job seemed to be more than he bargained for. He was climbing the ranks quickly, even getting a key to shut down for the night, but it was stressful and it added onto the stress that polluted his life recently. His mission there was tough, and it seemed to be moving at a snail's pace, but he would stay the course and hoped it would turn around quickly.

Mark sighed as he entered his car. It was finally time; he would go see Karen today at the hospital, even though she probably wouldn't have wanted to see him. He had kept putting it off.

He opened the notebook in his passenger seat and penned a note for her before he left.

Mark found the room that held Karen; she was hooked up to the beeping machines. She was a mess of tubes and laid there motionless. It took everything for him to be there. To finally do what he needed to.

Mark opened up her right hand; it was stiff and hardened, like she was already long gone. He put the note in her left hand and left. The note was written so she would wake up to know he was there for her in her darkest hour. It was to show that he never forgot her. She would know it all when she woke up.

If she woke up.

The Final Era

January 12th, 2014

A lifeless cadaver spearheads the frame. He was stunned. He didn't know what to do. What to say. How to act.

He wanted to run. He was good at running. He hated where he was and yet he would be hated if he left. He wanted to be alone…

David left the rehabilitation facility in the night. They wouldn't be able to save him, he knew that. It was time to leave it all behind. He searched his dreams, or were they visions? Memories? He didn't know. He never knew. He would never know. The secret of this side of him was never getting better. David was never able to take control of the dreams; they were too strong. They were for him, by him.

David's instinct took him to a graveyard. Why? He knew and yet he didn't. His mind took him here. His premonitions brought him here.

His mind took control of his legs as he walked up to the graveyard. The stone driving path served well as his walking path.

His mind forced a b-line from the stony path to the grass and straight for a tombstone. Which one? *You know.*

David fell to the ground in a seated position next to the tombstone. He looks left, with the gravestone in his peripheral vision. He tries to look directly at the name and fails; his head falls into his chest and everything he's ever felt starts to bubble over. The wind keeps swirling, maintaining a silent audience.

"What the hell do I-I even say to a gravestone?" David paused and tried to find something to utter.

"I've made a lot of mistakes and have a lot of regrets, but this," he points to the headstone, without looking, "this was the biggest one." If this was even this life, he thinks. "I ran and I ran, expecting this to go away, expecting this to get better without facing it, and it never did. Just like so many other things." David laughed despite himself.

"I wanted to move on from your death, like everyone said. They make it sound so easy, but we all know that's a farce. You never move on. The pain just keeps silently wearing and gnawing at you. You never move on from death. You never shake it. It always remains."

David looked up to see the gravestone. 'Meredith Veronica Renninger, 1929-1999.' It was this life. That seemed to be the case, at least.

"I was young and dumb. I know that and I still can't forgive myself. I won't. I don't deserve it. I deserve no forgiveness for anything I've done."

David starts to weep and through it all achieved some clarity. He knows what he has to do.

"I wasn't sure what I honestly came here to do, or what my mind wanted me to accomplish here. I don't feel like I'm in control of anything anymore... I don't know…" he laughed a hollow laugh, "but I realize now, that I'm not long for this world either. So I guess I'm here to try and mend fences a bit, even though you're dead and gone and have been for a while and can't hear me anyways. Or my dreams knew this was the only way to show me." This was his defining mistake. It was the only way he could have realized his fate. He was a failure. David looked up at the dead, gray sky. "These will be my last moments in this mortal coil. I've thought about it for a while but I know it now, after being here. I'd like to think I'll see you and everyone else in an afterlife, but I never really believed in that, especially after everything that has happened. I know you did, though. You deserve it, I always knew that, but I definitely don't."

David rose to his feet, knowing these would be his last days on this earth. He'll be free soon. The wind keeps swirling.

Act III: "Where Our Hearts Will Lie"

Daniel Drake

The Final Era

January 16th, 2014

The cold path becomes colder. The bitter path becomes even more bitter. He pushes on through the swirling winds.

The winds lick his face and stay unrelenting. The void of black is as close as ever. The ring of white still surrounds it. He extends his hand to it. He touches the black…

A whirlwind consumes his body. His fingers look mangled and twisted and contorted. Every part of him says to pull away, to turn back, but he doesn't.

Everything is wrong.

Everything is right.

This was it.

He pushes his hand even farther into the void; the blackness seems to salivate at the opportunity. He could almost hear it say 'finally'.

The time has come and it sucks him in completely. The void dissipates…

He wakes up paralyzed. Nothing surrounds him but he wonders if it's everything. Where was he? He starts to panic as he realizes his situation.

Daniel Drake

Perilous, suspended, floating in nothing. A black surrounds him. He can't move and he can't feel anything around him.

There was no light. He can't swim. He's all alone…

David stumbles down the corridor of a shady motel. It was carpeted red and had flickering lights. Every door looked like it hadn't been serviced since it was built.

He opened the door to Room 0720. It was a dark night, around midnight. The hail hit down in thumps on the windows. A nasty night with a nasty finish awaiting.

David sat on the bed turning over his past year. What all led to this. He was on top of the world. He was engaged to the girl of his dreams, he got the job of his dreams, and it was something that he could never get back. He didn't have the power or the energy to bring it back. Not that he ever could anyways. He didn't deserve it.

Everything fell apart. Liz died. His best friend. Sam, died. He fell into a pit that had no return. He went to alcohol. He went to drugs. He got put onto various medications with crippling side effects. He had no will left. Nothing left to give. A ghost walking in the aftermath.

David's marriage fell apart as a result. He was supposed to be five days married; he laughed hollowly. He was completely at fault. He wasn't there for her. He never helped her derelict heart. He couldn't perform, which led to her cheating. He met Mark and brought the Judas into his life. He hurt Karen and put her in a coma. It was all his fault. All of his life, or lives, was all on him.

The world turned its back on him. David was left to fight this alone and he deserved no less. From his personal life to his career. No one cared about him anymore and he could only blame himself.

He deserved to die. The world was better off without him. David couldn't take it anymore. He wanted, no, needed, to put an end to this once and for all. Never to return.

David went to the bathroom; it was as grimy as everything else in the facility. He grabbed a towel that probably hadn't been washed in centuries and wrapped it tightly around the shower curtain rod. He pulled the towel as hard as he could handle to test its strength; it would do.

He stood on the rim of the tub. Everything he was, every life he had lived, everything he had done came to this.

I hope I see everyone again, David thought, Sam, Liz, Grandma, and everyone in my dreams. I hope whoever is up there counts my mistakes and lets me in.

Who am I kidding? He thinks. There's nothing waiting for this wretch of a man.

He put his head through the towel. There's no time to go back. It was time for him to die. He takes a step off the rim and takes another. He dangles from the curtain rod.

Tonight, he was alone for the very last time…

January 17th, 2014: Beginnings Birthed by Endings, An Epilogue

Joyce received the call: David was gone. Well before the call, she felt it. She knew it. A half to a whole was now gone forever.

"...the fire, that originated at a mental health center, keeps raging across-" The transmission cut out; she wasn't sure exactly why.

The world kept falling. The world kept dying. It was a scourge. An epidemic. The past year brought more deaths than the Black Death. How many were left?

She didn't know what was happening entirely, even though it was starting to form in her mind's eye, but she knew it was merely the beginning.

Even through the endless suffering, Joyce unknowingly became stronger.

Karen woke up. She looked left to her bedside to find Mark holding a pillow to his chest for comfort.

"Hi, honey." She was still groggy, but he looked disheveled. Even with what he did, Karen still loved Mark greatly.

Mark smiled and pointed to the note.

"How sweet." She smiled weakly.

She opened it to find nothing scrawled. Karen looked up only to see white. Mark pressed the pillow down onto her head. The beeps faded slowly until they were completely nonexistent.

She was dead.

She served her purpose.

Mark left the room, suppressing any emotion that wasn't joy or triumph. He opened the bathroom door, leaned on the sink, and looked in the mirror. He smiled a broad smile as he thought about the great things he has accomplished.

Mark burned down the mental health facility; they were weak and useless anyways. They stood in his way. How smart was he to get himself employed there?

His bandmates. He never cared for them. It's always a nice trick to leave syringes around the people. It was almost too easy to make people think it was an accidental overdose.

Sam. He knew he was the key to take David down. All it took was the proper time to strike and the proper time was the death of Liz. He got him hooked on heroin and waited for him to expire. And then taking care of David was academic.

Mark looked closer at the face he's assumed and the hair he's cultivated. He pulled out a knife and sheared the messy, unkempt, almost afro-like hair. His hair reverted back to its normal black, short and slicked back. His face begins to shift back to its original form. Mark is no more.

A buzz from his IEM. "Sir, I just read the news." The voice says. "Another Entity is down."

"Yes." He continued to smile. "Only four more left to go."

"The world continues to fall. More deaths this past year than during a plague. The progenies are dying fast."

"It has come along nicely, hasn't it?"

"Are you ready for the next step?"

"Yes. Send me the names."

He will begin here, like he never left. This was his world, and her's (the memory of her scathed his mind), and he will take it back. It was just the beginning…

"Alright, David," he said to himself in the mirror, "let's finish what we started."

www.ingramcontent.com/pod-product-compliance
Lightning Source LLC
Chambersburg PA
CBHW061423160726
47995CB00003B/731